A soldier is summoned to the North Pole, days before the year changes, told to fix the great Clock for a celebration. He has no idea what to do.

A girl, hunted for the crime of being born, almost dies out on the ice. She is rescued by the last polar bear left alive.

A library waits for them both, a library built over a span of a hundred years, forgotten in the basement of an ice shack.

The world hasn't known hunger or sickness in hundreds of years. It has also forgotten love and beauty.

This is the One World.

The year is 2524.

Inspired by the short stories of Ray Bradbury, this futuristic young adult novel in three parts is set in a world where Christmas -among other things- is obsolete and a Clock is what keeps the fragile balance of peace.

Written in three parts, this is the breathtaking story of how two unlikely people change the world, and each other, one book at a time.

In *No Vain Loss*, the world is on the brink of the greatest war humanity has ever known. Lives will be lost. New truths will be revealed.

And nothing will ever be the same again.

Also by M.C. Frank

No Ordinary Star
NO ORDINARY STAR, PART ONE

No Plain Rebel
NO ORDINARY STAR, PART TWO

Ruined
a Regency romance

Lose Me.
a novel

Lowry and The Giver to Bradbury and The Illustrated Man and Pullman's His Dark Materials). -**Tracie Nicole**

A heartbreaking and lovely story. -**Joselyn Raquel MB**

There were some very Handmaid's Tale-esque references, particularly in reference to way women in this world are treated, and honestly, many of the thoughts I had while reading it are relevant to what's happening in the world today. -**Stef Galvin**, *The Novel Tea Corner*

A book I would reread over again! Perfectly written! -**PugReads**

An ode to scifi with a modern twist. –**Kat**, *Not The Path To Narnia*

I adore this novel and everything about it. –**Alexis**, *Mad For Books, Luv*

Absolutely smashing. -**Paperback_queen**

It's a mixture of science, romance, thrill, excitement and survival tactics. -**Shabnam**

As this story progressed I just wanted more and more. The writing blew me away again! The story is even more thrilling, and once you start reading you won't want to stop. –**Kelsey**, *Darcy's Book Blog*

No Ordinary Star is an immersive, fast paced story that reads like a dream. It is elegantly emotional and captivating. Prepare yourself for an astronomical amount of imagery. –**Adrienne**, *Darque Dreamer Reads*

It's official, I'm 100% an M.C. Frank fangirl, I'm convinced that she can do no wrong when it comes to storytelling. The world she has created is familiar yet unique, a world that could actually be a possibility in the future. Reminiscent of Ray Bradbury, M.C. weaves a tale that is equal parts hypnotic and horrifying. -**Kendall**, *The Geeky Yogi*

NO
VAIN
LOSS

NO ORDINARY STAR
PART THREE

M.C. FRANK

Title: No Vain Loss
Author: M. C. Frank

This book is a work of fiction. All names, characters, places and incidents are products of the author's imagination or are used fictitiously and are not to be construed as real. Any resemblance to actual events, locales, organizations, or persons living or dead, is entirely coincidental.

Inspired by the short stories of Ray Bradbury

and

dedicated to the person who taught me to love them.

In the end, you didn't make me hate the sun*. On the
night that you left there was a full moon.
I haven't looked at it since.

*Reference to a short story by Ray Bradbury,
'The Rocket Man'
from 'The Illustrated Man'

A guard steps in front of him, snatching him from his thoughts. Felix looks up and stifles a cry. The guard is looking down at him, his face filling Felix's vision. There's something familiar about the guard's face, and it feels to Felix that the floor tilts beneath his boots, because that face... That man...

It's not a guard at all; it's Luke.

For a second he's worried he was so lost in his thoughts he's beginning to see things. Luke gives him a small smile and winks.

"Ready?" he asks.

It *is* him. It is Luke. His eyes are the same as the last time he saw him, alert and smiling, but he's dressed in a Guard's uniform. How the timers did he-?

Without waiting for an answer, Luke walks over to the panels and presses a button. On the PR screen, Felix watches as the crowd gasps. The huge dome over their heads collapses in on itself, folding in half, dissolving in front of their eyes. They all tip their heads back, staring at the shimmering nanos that change positions and shift and sparkle until there's nothing left but the midnight sky above their heads.

"That's it," Luke says, calmly, as though it's no big deal what he just did. As though it's no big deal, opening the merking Dome of the Stadium. "Now the men are free to walk in and defend you, should you need them to. The rest is up to you, prince boy. Mark will keep the dome down for as long as he can..."

The Rebel steals a glance at Felix's frozen face and frowns.

"Act normal, all right?" another voice tells him. "No one will know this wasn't planned, not yet. Everyone will assume someone up higher gave the order for the Dome to come down.

There's another Rebel beside him; Felix didn't notice him at first, but now that the Rebel turns to give him an encouraging nod, he realizes who he is. He's one of them, too. Oh. He's the hacker. He must be Mark.

"Go get them," Luke says, giving him a little push.

Felix stumbles, then shakes his head to clear it.

What is happening?

The Rebels must have infiltrated the Stadium and hacked into the Dome's system. There must be more spread around the Stadium, dressed like the Chairman's Guard.

I'm not alone.

Felix has no idea what he's doing. Luke pushes him again until his legs are standing on a round little platform. Then Mark passes his hand, palm down, over the panel, and the platform begins to ascend slowly.

Felix tips his head back and he can see, from the sky, the 2525 year's Clock being lowered exactly on top of him. For a second they float towards each other, Felix and the Clock, coming from two opposite directions, calculated to meet at the exact same time. The middle of the stage is empty, waiting for them.

Chairman Kun is in his seat, like everyone else, just a head in the immense crowd.

The round platform emerges on the stage and fastens into place with a soft click.

The Clock is floating a few meters off the ground, just above Felix's head, so that it can be visible from every angle. Felix tries to breathe.

He finds the button inside his cloak and presses it.

His heart gives a huge thump.

The large hand of the Clock moves towards the 12. He's done it, it's working. His heart is synchronized with the Clock. While he was taking the pills, his heart wasn't supposed to be ticking like a human heart at all. But that's over now; it's started beating. Beating and thumping and racing. After a breath, his heart will beat again, and the hand will move again with it.

The crowd watches the Clock in fascination, holding its breath, waiting for the spectacle to begin. Felix's heart beats in a slower frequency than seconds, but nobody has any idea how a heart beats -or how a clock ticks, for that matter- so at least that buys him some time.

Not much, though.

It's ten heartbeats to midnight.

t w o

Right. Relax, you've got this.

Felix is talking to himself now. That's what he's been reduced to, he who was once the best lieutenant of his year. His brain, which was designed to be the most highly-intelligent lethal weapon on Earth, has forgotten how to work properly. It's frozen. All it can do is count down the crazy things he has done in the past few days.

He has left his regiment, abandoned his squad, gone off the grid. Right now he's wanted by the military, and not just by them. He's wanted by the Chairman of the One World himself.

He has spent the past ten days in an ice shack in the Arctic, listening to the messages of a possibly crazy old man who says he was his grandfather.

He has stopped taking the pills, but he's still alive. He's eaten food. Real food.

He's met a girl. A girl with hair the color of fire. He's touched her. He's saved her life. He's saved Astra's life. More than once. And she's saved his.

He's cried.

He's laughed.

He didn't know any of these things existed before he watched the merking Clockmaster's message. He didn't know he could do any of them. Well, most of them are illegal. A few are punishable by death. But still, it felt so good. To smile, to use his head, to talk, to learn. To hurt. Actually, that didn't feel good at all. But it felt real. Real as the flame of the match Astra lit to save their lives the day he met her.

Real as the snow on the mountainside where he met Luke and the other Rebels.

Real as the voice of the Clockmaster when he explained to him everything: how the Chairman sold the Earth to the Counsil of the One World and plotted with the Commander of Venus to destroy its population with a virus inside the huge Clock. The Clock he's about to deliver to the Perennial Celebration.

Felix turns around and grabs the bottom part of the disc of the Clock. Immediately it's lowered -the techs downstairs must be watching his every move, guessing his every command before he'll even need to voice it. The Clock is brought down until the ballerina and the one-legged soldier Astra drew in its middle are almost level with his head.

Now what?

Go get them.

Easier said than done. The Stadium is filled to the brim with people. Hundreds of thousands of them, seated across from him, above him, to the left, to the right, behind his back. An entire amphitheatre packed with them. And he's standing in the small platform in the middle of it all, all eyes on him.

Any moment now, Felix is supposed to reveal the Clock that's going to ring in the new year. The year 2525.

The year the End will begin.

And he's the only one who can stop it. He wasn't supposed to be alone. He and Astra started it together, but she's not here to finish it.

He's lost her. But he's found something else: the truth. Or at least the beginning of it.

Relax, for merc's sake. Don't think about that right now. You're no use for anything if you're not calm; the entire plan will be blown.

The Elite guests of the Perennial have no idea that the crystal Dome has actually disappeared above their heads. No one is protesting as yet about the missing ceiling and walls -Luke and the Rebels hacked the system and collapsed the round structure of the Perennial Site and now the guests' heads are exposed to the arctic night, but they seem to think it's part of the Celebration. The sky above is clear, no snowflakes in sight, so the guests think it's all part of the show. Still, Felix wonders that the technicians don't realize that the system override is a hack. Maybe such a thing is unthinkable in the well-ordered universe that surrounds the Chairman and all he controls.

To some extent that's true, he knows it now. But then how did the Rebels get in here? And what do they think they're...?

"What the timers are you doing?" a voice hisses at him from downstairs.

Felix almost jumps a foot in the air. That's *her* voice. Her words. And he didn't hear them inside his head this time. She's here. He looks down carefully, concealing his face inside the cloak's hood.

There, between his boots, is a small gap in the platform, through which he can see the below-stage room, where the techs and stage hands are running around, taking care of every detail that keeps the huge Dome and the amphitheatre up and running. Then he sees it: the source of the voice. There's a person standing directly below him.

No, that can't be right. He looks up again, trying to concentrate on the Clock.

"Pssst."

What the merc?

There, right below him. A flash of red.

He moves his foot a little, so that he can see beyond the hole in the platform. He sees a glimpse of her hair first, glowing as it catches a thin ray of light from the Stadium.

Then he sees the rest of her.

His heart leaps to his throat.

He bends on one knee, letting the cloak billow dramatically around his boots, and pretends he's fixing a circuit in the corner of the Clock.

"Astra," he whispers, blinking, trying to clear his vision.

She -because it *is* her, unbelievable as it is- looks up at him, a question in her green eyes.

"What?" she mouths. "Tell me you have a plan."

What plan? Oh, right, the plan. He nods.

"Do something for me?" he whispers down to her. His voice echoes all the way below-stage. *You're here*, he keeps thinking. *You're here.* He fixes Astra with his eyes, hoping she'll understand what he needs her to do, without him having to explain.

He has no idea how he manages to stay sane and keep breathing, since there's a lump the size of the Dome lodged in his throat.

It's her. She's here. Who knows how the Rebels managed it, but they did. He told them he needed her and they got her to him. Simple as that.

He can't keep his lips from breaking into a huge smile as he's looking down at her. She's standing right beneath the little platform opening, dressed in the green and white hand-crafted cotton Rebel clothes. She looks clean and rested and well-fed. Her face is upturned as she's looking up at him.

Her cheeks look pale in the dim light, contoured by that cloud of red hair, which is sort of tamed in a braid, hanging down over her left shoulder. She looks concentrated and prepared. And beautiful as merc. His whole body is shaking with the need to be close to her.

"Anything," she whispers up at him.

He quickly leans down, reaching an arm to her, and she grabs it. Her hands feels small within his, cool, steady. He's reminded of the day he pulled her from the icy water, although now she's the one doing the rescuing.

He pulls her up on the stage next to him in a split second, looping an arm around her waist and lifting her bodily next to him as though she's weightless, and deposits her on her feet.

The audience is silent. They aren't freaking out at the mere sight of a woman and a man standing next to each other, they aren't running down the aisles towards them, guns aimed at their hearts. Yet. So far so good.

Felix takes a split second to catch his breath, and then takes a step forward, closing the distance between himself and Astra. He places a hand on her right elbow.

"You're not going to like this, match girl," he murmurs and she has barely a second to look at him in shock. Then he leans forward and presses his lips to hers.

Later he'll wonder whether she knew, when she gave him her hand, that she was walking into certain death. And didn't care.

Later he'll also wonder what on mars he was thinking about while her kiss was burning a hole on his lips, because he sure as merc wasn't thinking of the war they're starting. He *should* have -he should have been thinking of his next move.

Right now he should be organizing his thoughts, buying time; that had been his plan. But he isn't.

That's why he'd asked the Rebels to give him Astra, and he would take care of everything. That's why he'd told them: "she is the match."

She was the plan, all along.

The plan had been that he'd kiss her and their Felony would shock everyone out of their pills-induced drone-like state. The plan had been that he'd kiss her and gain some time to think. The plan had been that he'd kiss her and it wouldn't be a big deal that they broke the law for either of them, since they are both already wanted criminals, sentenced to death. The plan had been that he'd kiss her and the soldiers would kill him then and there, and the Perennial wouldn't proceed, so the virus wouldn't be released, and so the Earth wouldn't be destroyed. Or, maybe, while he was kissing her, he would have time to think for a way to save them both.

Maybe while the Elite witnessed the kiss, something everyone forgot even exists, something unknown and forbidden, something he himself only recently read about, he would be preparing to face his worst enemy, the Chairman of the One World, his father. That had been the plan.

But that's not how it goes. He hadn't counted on what kissing does to your brain: it turns it into mush, apparently. Maybe that's why it's illegal.

Right now all he can think about is the way her lips part under his and how his whole body lights up like a match as her palm moves to rest lightly on his back. Where should he put his hands? He slowly raises one to her hair -he's always wanted to do that, from the first moment he carried her, half-frozen, to Ulysses' shack, and it was just a dark mass of hair, plastered to her forehead, dripping all over his uniform. Now he buries his fingers in it, shutting his eyes as its silky texture meets his skin, running his hand down the length of the thick braid that hangs like a rope down her back. He cups her neck first with one, then both hands, lifting her face to his. Then he can't think anymore.

Astra feels warm in his arms, her body soft against his chest, her mouth opening beneath his. He tastes colors on her tongue, all the brilliant colors she brought into his life. His chest is exploding with a million feelings he didn't know existed, and his body can barely contain them.

There's an ache throbbing inside his chest, at the place where his heart is beating crazily, and it's getting to be so excruciating that he gasps against her lips. He wants to climb out of his own skin and into hers -that's the only way his chest will stop feeling hollow.

She sighs against his lips and he feels his knees begin to give way. He parts his legs slightly, so that he'll have a larger base to stand on as he's supporting Astra's weight, balancing her waist on his hips, lifting her practically off her feet. He still has to bend his head down to reach hers though, which makes it a bit difficult for their mouths to fit. He turns his head to the left so that his chin is under hers, curling his fingers across the slope of her neck, and her taste explodes in his mouth.

Oh, that's how their heads are supposed to go.

He didn't know that before.

He had no idea that a human's face is built to fit exactly with another's for a kiss. Who knows what else it can fit for? Who knows...?

Ah. She's found his tongue. Stars, what is she doing to him? His whole brain is on fire. His skin feels too tight. She raises herself on tiptoes and buries her fingers in the wisps of hair at the nape of his neck. Her lips move against his mouth and he has to fight to keep his knees from buckling. His hands slide to her hips and he feels her sag against him, boneless. He pulls her to him fiercely, obliterating any space between them.

"Ash," he gasps against her mouth. "Astra..." He's shaking so much he can barely get her name out. He forgets everything around them, wanting only to meld his body to hers, to keep their lips touching forever.

His heart is beating like crazy and the seconds on the Clock are tumbling together unevenly.

The crowd is absolutely still -not that he gives a merc, but they are. Then again, they didn't even notice the protective Dome folding to nothing around them, leaving them exposed to the crisp Arctic air. And they don't seem to notice either when Felix's heart gives a loud thump and the Clock's hands move. The Clock, connected to Felix's heartbeat, rings in the new year with one powerful strike of its match-hands.

It's officially twelve o' clock.

The year 2525 has begun. Only no one's attention is on that.

There's no celebration, no voices joining in the 'One World' salute chant, nothing. Just gaping, horrified silence. A few guards have moved closer to the platform, guns at the ready, but so far no one has given them a direct order.

Felix himself has no idea what's going on around them.

He doesn't have a clue that he just brought in the new year. He'd never realize it at all, in fact, if it wasn't for Astra shuddering in his arms and drawing away, taking a step back and then another, until she's standing on her own. His eyes stay glued to her face. He lifts his hand and trails a finger on the line of her jaw, up where it meets her ear, and she freezes. Her skin is burning his knuckles, her breath coming short. *Good thing she can breathe through all of this*, he thinks, *because I sure as merc have forgotten how to.* He feels as if he needs to jump out of his skin.

Then Astra does the last thing he expects her to do -but then again, isn't that what she's been doing from the start?

"Are you done?" she whispers into his lips.

What? His brain needs a second to process the meaning of her words. *Did she say 'are you done?'* That can't be right.

"Felix," Astra says. "They're here."

Oh. That's when he wakes up, brutally.

He takes a hasty step away from her, stumbling, but her hands circle his waist and she steadies him invisibly, hiding the movement inside the pooling folds of his black cloak.

He gasps and tries to take a breath, his lips brushing against her chin. "Help me," he whispers as he did the day he met her.

Without even looking down, he can tell she's smiling. He feels the movement of her lips against his cheek as her whole face stretches into the smile.

Finally, he thinks. *I got a smile out of her.*

And then all hell breaks loose.

three

From his seat in the front row, among the Counsil Members, Chairman Kun flicks his hand. That's all it takes for the guards to flood the lanes of the Stadium towards Felix and Astra and circle them within seconds. There's the sound of their boots shuffling on the glass floors. People start to scream as soon as they see the guards running with guns bared, but the Chairman keeps his seat calmly, his gaze fixed on the two figures on the performing platform, steely but detached. Felix lifts his head from Astra's, his left hand already stealing to his thigh, to the Protector .44 that's strapped to his Hydro suit.

In a second, Astra's cool palm is on top of his.

Her eyes are still on his. *No*, they say. *Focus. You're awake now. A bullet is not the solution to everything.*

And then they don't say anything anymore, because one of the guards reaches them, his hand outstretched. Before Felix can turn his head to take a good look at the guard, Astra's jumped in front of him, flinging an arm out to shield him.

The guard's rod, going for his upper arm, finds the side of her neck instead, and latches itself onto the soft, warm skin that was pressed against his palm a second ago: Astra's throat. His fingers were right at that spot, trailing the delicate crevice between her collarbones. But now, the taser buries itself into her flesh and she starts convulsing, her small body shaking violently, her teeth gritted to keep in the screams. Her eyes find his for an instant before rolling back in her head and then she's falling.

There's no time to react.

Felix just watches, horrified, as the guard buries his taser-rod into her skin again, and the life leaves her body with a shuddering breath. She topples to the floor so abruptly he doesn't have time to blink. His gun clatters to the ground as he leaps to cradle her head with his hand and her body hits the platform with a sickening, hollow bang. He drops to his knees next to her.

The Stadium explodes with noise, but it all fades to the background. The people's faces blur together, they cease to exist. Felix's movements get slow as though he's underwater.

No, his brain screams. *This can't be happening. Get up. Get up get up get up.*

But Astra just lays there, her hand curled at an unnatural angle underneath her head, her red hair spilled over his fingers.

four

A weight is pressing down on Felix's chest as he bends over her, struggling to take a breath, but choking instead. He's shaking her, calling her name in an endless loop inside his head, but no sound is coming out.

"No!" someone screams, a hoarse sound, as though their insides are being torn to a million pieces. The voice is his own, but he doesn't recognize it. "No. Nononononono. Astra, come on, open your eyes. *Ash!*"

Help me, he'd told her.

"Not this way, Ash, I didn't mean…" He swears, and is surprised to hear his voice crack. "Come on, match girl, come on."

He places his hands, fingers outstretched, on her chest, intending to pump life back into her just like he'd done the day she almost died in the shack, but there's no time.

Hands grab him as more guards bend down, dragging her body away from him. He struggles to keep her close, but they're many and he is one. He's feeling her slip away from him, her waist wrenched from between his hands, her braid stretched out on the sleek floor.

For merc's sake, Felix thinks at her savagely, only this time she won't think anything back. For merc's sake, don't leave me to fight alone! You should have let them taser me, kill me, if you were going to destroy me anyway.

The guards force him upright so that he's standing -when did he drop to his knees? He hadn't noticed. All he can see is that they're taking her body from him. His head is filled with fog. His body sags; he's got no strength to fight against the arms that are constraining him.

"Aaaaaaaah!"

Out of nowhere this low, rumbling war cry sounds, and everyone turns their heads to see where it's coming from. The glass trembles with the scream's resonance, and a guard runs up to the stage so fast he's practically a blur, flinging himself onto the soldiers that are holding Astra. Surprised, they stand back, letting her lifeless body slide to the floor.

The guard growls some more -he looks young, but his movements are sure and deliberate, as though he's been trained well and hard. He stands over Astra's body, his chest heaving, placing a foot on either side of her crumpled form and letting his arms hang loosely by his sides. His muscles are flexing and his fists are lightly clenched as though he's ready to fight anyone who would dare come near her.

He lifts his gaze to Felix.

"What...?" Felix's heart stops. *Merc.* The 'guard' is no guard at all. He's another one of the Rebels. He remembers him; he's younger than the others, closer to Astra's age. He kept looking at him with eyes cold with mistrust back at their camp.

Now his eyes are wild as he falls to his knees, quickly wiping the hair away from her cheeks.

"Leave her alone!" the words almost burst from Felix's lips, but he stops himself in time.

He feels a rage wake up inside him and a tremor travels down his body. *How dare the Rebel touch her? How dare he? Even now that she's...* He can barely keep himself from lunging for the Rebel's neck, but at least he's woken up from that damned stupor of losing her. He stands up tall, wrestling his arms from the guards' iron grip. He's got the long, muscled body of a well-trained soldier, and yet here he is, struggling to gather his thoughts, let alone coordinate his movements to fight his captors. The white- blond streak of hair that marks him as a lieutenant of the One World's Army falls into his eyes and he flips it to the side impatiently.

What is this thing that's erupting within him? Does this rage have a name?

Why does he suddenly want to drop everything, to forget about the Chairman and the Commander of Venus and their plans, and wrench the Rebel's hands away from Astra's still shoulders? Is he going mad?

Is the match girl making him crazy even after she's gone?

By this point, the rest of the guards have caught up to the fact that something is wrong with this "guard" who's acting as crazy as if he's got the After Plague. They grab the Rebel roughly to pull him back and away from Astra, and hoist him to his feet with force. But before he's yanked away, his eyes snap to Felix. His lips move. "Go on," the Rebel mouths to him, a frantic expression on his face, a question in his eyes.

What are you hesitating for? That's what it looks like he's silently wondering.

If Felix knew the reason himself, he'd get rid of it. But he doesn't. A dark feeling of emptiness settles in the pit of his stomach, taking the place of the rage. He's used to be the best of the best, but now he fells inadequate, helpless... Worthless. An overwhelming desire to step aside and let the Rebels take over sweeps over him. They would do a much better job than him.

He knows suddenly what that rage was, that envy. All he can think of is, *Astra grew up with this boy. He probably caught fish, actual, edible, fat fish for her to eat, and slept next to her in their caves and sat with her listening to Steadfast's plans.*

This Rebel boy is so different from him... *He* wouldn't freak out at the mere sight of real flames, like he, Felix, did. Felix would bet that *he* never pointed a gun at Astra; in fact, he's never pointed a gun at the wrong person, period. He must have loved the light as much as she, never forced her to stay in a closed space because that's how he'd been taught to feel safe. He'd never have Astra faint on him, because he ate all the timer biscuits like an ass. He may even have handled a rescued book before, maybe read something to her on top of a mountaintop, understanding every word that was written. He was never blind and asleep and stupid; he was never a Drone.

No wonder she ran away from Felix to go to the Rebel camp. No wonder he couldn't save her. He's worthless.

The Stadium takes a sudden dip to the left. Felix tries to clear his vision, but something cold and heavy is pressing on his chest, stealing his breath. Everything goes black for a split second.

For a moment, he thinks he'll collapse on his face on the floor right there, in front of Kun and the Rebel and the thousands of guests -as though he hasn't already made enough of a spectacle of himself, screaming Astra's name like that...

A sharp pain jolts him from his thoughts. His head is being bent roughly to the side, and someone is fumbling with his black hood to get his neck exposed.

Kun orders his head chopped off. Turns out, five seconds are plenty.

Felix knew beforehand that he wouldn't be allowed to play the PR to the end, but for the first few seconds everyone is so surprised that they just stand there, guards and guests alike, and listen. On the fringes of the Stadium, on the slopes leading down to the upper seats, he can barely discern a few lone silhouettes, just dots walking towards the Dome on the white snow, the Perennial Site lights casting long shadows behind them. Are they there for him?

He's not sure he actually sees them. It might be a trick of the light. He doesn't dare hope.

In the sound-Vis, Ulysses is still firing sentences like shots. He's said the most important stuff already, and he's now getting to the point where he's describing the way the Clock is supposed to work, spreading the virus, spreading death. As he sees Kun starting to get up, Felix springs to action.

He brings one hand behind his head and flings his hood back. The motion reminds him of that time on the ice when he bit his glove off to grab Astra's frozen little hand before she was submerged forever. The day he started taking off the straps of the One World that were choking him, keeping him asleep, blind, stupid. His glove must be still there, near the icy lake, buried somewhere beneath the snow.

Much good he did to Astra, saving her. He ended up killing her.

'No need for thanks,' she'd told him. *'I'll save you right back.'*

"I am Felix Delta Chi, the head of Chairman Kun's Scouting Office Net," he improvises a lie, feeling a little silly, but nobody interrupts him, so he goes on, "and as such I'm accusing him of high treason against the Planet of Earth and all the Colonies!"

Only then does Kun speak for the first time -and not to him. He doesn't even give any indication that he has recognized Felix's name or face. He addresses his Guard, ignoring Felix, ignoring the accusation, even ignoring the stupid fake title Felix gave himself.

"Proceed," Kun's calm voice says and the guards take a step closer to Felix.

The Chairman is obscured from Felix's vision by the guard's backs, but he doesn't need to see his face to know he's fully aware of what's happening. Perhaps he's the only one. He sure as merc recognized Astra, and even if he didn't recognize his own son, the 'Felix' must have done it. Or at least the initials of the non-existent Scouting Office Net. Which spell 'son'.

By now some kind of silent alarm must have been raised, and it's beyond possible that reinforcements will be arriving at any moment from all over the Planet's military bases. No time to waste -but Felix knew that already, seeing as two guards are reaching for his neck again and the rest have pulled their guns out and are aiming them at his chest.

"Wait!" he calls.

Again, they obey. Which makes him think. Why the stars would they obey the orders of the man they've been told to kill? Is there something that makes them... obedient? Prone to suggestion?

Could it be the same thing that made his heart silent, that made his thoughts empty and his mind calm? That day that Astra threw the last of his pills to the fire, when she said that 'they were poison', could her words have had more than one meaning? Could it be that the Health Discs-?

He doesn't get to finish his thought, because right then, two things happen simultaneously.

The first is that it starts to snow. Felix realizes it when he feels something wet land on the tip of his nose and lifts his eyes to the heavens. The snowflakes must have been drifting from the pitch-black sky for some time now, because he takes a small step and discovers the stage is sleek with ice. He looks around him. The guests are starting to stare upwards, to the dark, white-speckled sky, trying to fathom what this new trick is and finding that it's not as pleasant as the previous years' festivities, because it stings and melts on their clothes and hair.

Felix is watching the Chairman's reaction. At first, there's a slight frown on his smooth forehead. Then his eyes flicker with something like fear. Maybe he thinks it's the virus being sprinkled over the stadium after all, and he hasn't had time to make his escape. Felix's eyes narrow.

Let's see what you do about this, Felix thinks. *Let's see how you handle snow.*

He hasn't forgotten how he himself 'handled' it at first. Which was not well at all, but of course there was Astra there to... *No. Don't think about her now. You'll fall apart later. If there is a later.*

Then, before anyone has the chance to recover from the shock of the falling snow and the voice of Ulysses accusing his own son of the highest treason, the second miracle happens.

Astra opens her eyes.

Her head is right beside Felix's left boot, because he didn't budge an inch away from her body no matter how close the guards got to him. While everyone's staring at the Clock, he tears his eyes away from the blue-black snow plains that may or may not be bringing him help, and stares down at her face. He must be imagining it -he's almost sure he does.

He imagines her eyes blinking slightly, long eyelashes casting shadows on pale cheeks, pink lips opening to let out a sigh and a small, dry cough, as she's trying to catch her breath. Then he's no longer imagining it, or he is, but he's gone stark-raving mad, because her eyes open wide and stare back into his.

Her eyes widen and at first he thinks it's shock at seeing him surrounded by guards, guns to his throat. Then a vein starts throbbing on her forehead. She tries to lift her head but her neck won't obey her, and he finally snaps out of the shock.

Felix's entire body turns into a lit match; his heart gives a thud and tries to leap out of his chest. Stars, it's not his imagination, she *did* open her eyes. He looks down, his eyes burning.

She's not dead. She's dying.

"Breathe," he mouths, willing his body to stay still.

Astra takes a shuddering breath, and her eyes go dull. He knows that look. She's in pain. No, she's not in pain -she's in agony. He can see the skin on her neck, as she tries to turn her head slightly, right where the guard's rod went, and he has to turn away for a second, because pain sears his heart like a knife and he can't draw breath. The skin around her throat has bubbled up, fried, already turning black with third degree burns where the electricity entered her veins when they tasered her. Just like they did her father. Just like they killed Steadfast.

Astra swallows with difficulty and sends him a glance beneath furrowed eyebrows.

What? he thinks at her.

Stop staring at me, her eyes say.

Everything is happening within seconds, even though it feels like eons. On the PR, Ulysses starts the abbreviated version of how the Commander of Venus came to see his son. Astra lets out a small whimper that breaks Felix's heart in two. But that's not all the whimper does. It draws the attention of one of the guards who, seeing her wake up, bends down.

"Don't merking *touch* her," Felix mutters through clenched teeth. He whips around and plants a tight fist on the guard's jaw, who lands on his back on the slippery surface of the platform, sliding a few steps away. Before anyone has time to even blink once, Felix has grabbed Astra by the waist, and they've jumped through the trap-door, down to the dim-lighted pit.

He doesn't even wait for the platform to move beneath his weight, he just gathers his knees and lets himself fall, one hand behind Astra's head, the other stretched out to keep his balance. He lands below-stage in a crouch, and pushes himself to his feet in one fluid motion.

As soon as his feet touch the ground, a guard that's been left below-stage plants himself in his path, but Felix doesn't even stop. He just knees the guard in the stomach, lifting his leg in the air and then kicking his left ankle from under him. The tech hands scatter towards the tangle of tunnels that form the below-stage -they're not trained soldiers, after all, and much as they fear the Chairman's displeasure they're not about to get beat up by a lunatic when it's not their job to stop him.

"Ash," Felix whispers into Astra's head, his voice thick with tears. "Please..." his voice breaks. He's panting, although it's not from running, and pauses for just a moment, lifting a hand to smooth the hair away from her eyes. "Please don't hurt so bad. Just hold on. Hold on." He glances around quickly, and sees an opening to his left. He runs towards it.

He can't stand to think what the little gasps Astra is giving mean; he can't bear to even imagine what kind of pain she must be in. His vision blurs and he tells himself firmly to get a grip, while his eyes keep looking around frantically for Luke - for any of the Rebels.

"This way!" Luke is suddenly there, his hand warm on Felix's shoulder, and Felix starts running blindly to the direction he's leading him.

Astra is not resisting in his arms, not screaming at him to let her run on her own like a normal person, or looping her arm around his neck as he's carrying her. He knows it's bad.

They reach the door -it's closed, of course- and it's only then that Felix realizes he's been left alone for several minutes, ever since he jumped down from the platform with Astra. The below-stage pit is huge, and he's crossed it undisturbed.

He did run, but he's not even winded. He turns around quickly to see what's going on and he understands why.

The Rebels are here, behind him. He can see at least seven of them engaged in hand-to-hand combat with the guards, blocking their progress as they drop down from the stage trap one after one. They've lowered the Rebel boy who was tasered too. He's lying in a corner, his face tight and grayish, but he's already woken up and is flexing his fingers, itching to grab his gun. Luke and Matt are side by side, planting punches in the guards' faces, ducking exploding guns left and right. So far not one of the guards has managed to penetrate the wall the Rebels' bodies are making.

Felix starts to push his weight into the door, trying to get it to open.

"There's a button, tin soldier," Astra's voice says, breathless, from his chest.

"Hey," he murmurs, so glad she's able to speak, he doesn't even mind about being called a 'tin soldier'. To be honest, he kind of missed it. He pushes the button, and they're out.

A blast of cold air assaults them, and he closes his arms over Astra's head, trying to protect her from it. He takes in a sharp breath, shutting his eyes for a brief instant. Holding her feels so familiar, so safe. What doesn't feel so safe is the line of guards that's forming a hundred yards ahead, and especially the thin, tall silhouette in the middle. Kun.

The Chairman himself is coming after him; that's as bad as it gets.

But secretly, Felix is glad. So the Rebels did disable the Pods inside of the Stadium, otherwise the Chairman and his guards would have made their escape immediately. Instead, he's still here. Even from a distance, Felix can see that his father doesn't look too happy about it. More like murderous. The line of guards keeps advancing towards Felix and Astra, their steps muffled by the thick snow. Behind Felix the clamor of the Rebels' fighting fades, as the Dome's door drifts closed.

It's only them and the snow.

The Stadium's huge, bright light projectors cast everything in a bluish glow, as if it's early afternoon in the dark plain. A circle of light spreads all the way from the Stadium and fades towards the higher slopes of the mountains.

Felix shifts Astra's weight in his arms, supporting her head on his shoulder.

"Felix," she says, lifting warm brown eyes up to his. He focuses on her chapped lips, and all he can think of is how she tasted -how soon he can fit his own there again. "I'm not going back to the Box."

His heart gives a painful thud, and for a second he can't speak. He can hardly breathe.

"Not as long as I exist," he tells her in a strangled voice. "I'll take you to Mercury first."

"I'm not going to Mercury with you, no-brains," she replies, her voice a croak. "I'm not going anywhere with you."

Felix laughs and it sounds a bit watery, but still as much of a laugh as it possibly can. The black line of guards is about ten steps away now. He won't let her go from his arms. He doesn't have anything to fight with, or at least he doesn't have anything *better* to fight with.

"Keep talking like that and I might drop you," he says.

"Keep talking like that and I might punch you," she replies. Her breath catches.

"How do you feel?" he asks her immediately. "Are you ok?"

"Of course I'm not ok," she says and he grits his teeth. "I'm mad," she adds.

"What?" he says, taken by surprise, and she tries to laugh but ends up choking on a rasping breath. He lifts her against him, one arm across her shoulders, to help ease her breathing.

"I've only just found you," she says as soon as she can breathe, her voice the sound of sadness. "And already I'm leaving."

Felix stumbles, even though he wasn't walking.

He settles her in his arms, noticing the teardrops that are sparkling on her lashes. "Astra..." he begins, but he can't go on.

"I know I've been a burden to you," she says, her voice thick with tears. "I've known it from the start. It's always been like this, you know? It's the same for a lot of people. That's all we are on this Planet, unnecessary waste. You can go anywhere you want in the One World in moments, but no one really communicates, if you think about it; we do things -well, you men do things, but you don't really feel anything. No one does. Animals are something we feed into our labs, losing entire species without a second thought; women and girls the same. In the Box, what they did to us..."

Felix shudders at the tone of her voice, his arms going numb for a second, almost dropping her. His brain is racing back to the time he found her suffocating in her sleep, lost in a nightmare. He'd been scared that if he hadn't jerked her awake, she'd have fallen to pieces.

"You," she goes on, "you made me feel as though I was worth something, even though you didn't have to."

Felix freezes, his body tensing. "Is that what you think?" he mumbles, hardly knowing what he's saying. Is that what this Planet has taught her to think, this Planet with its military schools and university facilities for boys and worker's settlements for girls?

"It's what you thought, too," she replies.

Is it possible for a human being as exceptional as she to feel like this, to think that she's a burden, worthless, unwanted? Angry tears blind his vision.

"What did you say?" bursts from his lips in a furious whisper. "Didn't I ask you never to talk about yourself in that way in front of me? You couldn't be more wrong. And the ones who made you think of yourself like... like those words you just said... I don't want to repeat them. They're wrong, too. Criminally wrong. You're worth everything. You..." He shuts his eyes and rests his chin on her head, taking a big gulp of freezing arctic air. A few snowflakes wander inside his mouth as well, and he relishes their taste, swallowing their coldness.

"Did you know Kun and Constantine was one and the same person? That Kun is Ulysses' son and my father?"

"Yes."

He hoists her higher up in his arms, getting a firmer grip. The line of soldiers is closing in on them, but they still haven't opened fire. They want to waste as few bullets as they can. It will be over in seconds.

"The Rebels told me at some point," Astra says. "I'm sorry you had to find out from Ulysses' Vis. Are you mad I didn't tell you?"

He looks at her, incredulous. "Are you serious? If you're not mad that the Chairman's son has his arms around you, then how could I...?"

"Well, I have no choice, have I?" She interrupts him before he has time to finish his sentence. She coughs and shudders and he wraps his arms around her more tightly. "Are they going to kill us?"

Felix snorts. *Are they going to kill us?* What can he answer to that? He could tell her that of the things they could do to them, killing them is the best option. But he can't. And he doesn't have to anyway, because she knows. And there isn't a thing he can do to save her or himself.

"Stars take it," he mutters.

He shifts her weight in his arms, and squares his shoulders. He takes a step forward.

This is it. This is the exact moment when Felix Hunter, star lieutenant of the Intergalactic Armies of the One World, grandson of the Clockmaster and son of the traitor Chairman Kun, decides to fight. He had decided already, or so he thought, but the truth is he had made that decision with his brain only. He had thought and calculated and decided. Nothing like that happens inside his head now. With Astra secure in his arms, he begins advancing towards Kun and his men.

He hears the door burst open behind him, and someone -Luke?- screaming: "On your marks! On your marks! Get down. Hunter, watch out!" but he doesn't even turn to look. His heart explodes from his chest, jumping to meet Kun as he's walking towards him, head held low, eyes glowing in the darkness, flanked by twenty of his personal guards on either side. He just follows it.

It will lead him to death, and his brain knows that, but what he's only just finding out is that when your heart beats, when it beats strongly -if not entirely regularly- and more importantly when it beats next to the heart of the one person in the Planets who makes you come alive… Then you just follow. Come what may.

five

What comes, a second later, is Chairman Kun's Slayer .34, pointing directly at Felix's forehead. The Chairman's blue eyes, up close, are cool, calculating the distance between them as he takes a final step forward and presses the trigger.

In the split second before the gun explodes next to his temple, Felix opens his eyes wide to meet the icy stare of his father, wanting him to see the change in his own. Wanting to die with the knowledge that his father saw that he, Felix, has woken up.

But the explosion of pain never comes.

Next thing he knows, a huge black form is tumbling through the ranks of Kun's guards. He can't discern what it is, because it's coming from the shadows, beyond the Perennial lights. Whatever it is, it bursts in an avalanche of snow behind Kun's guards, like an immense cloud of darkness.

The Dome is lit up like a sun, all its doors shut, and Felix with his cadets are standing a few steps in front of it. Kun and his guards are coming down from the other side of the plain, and Felix is trapped, he has nowhere to go. But all this changes within seconds.

The dark form erupts behind the ranks of Kun's soldiers, moving so fast it's like a blur, and it's so huge that its mere size is sending most of the men flying to the ground and a few running in terror. The rest are trampled underneath it.

"Stand down! Soldiers stand down!" a general's voice yells, from Kun's side.

Then a massive howl shatters the night and a massive, white form bursts from behind the fallen guards, spraying a shower of snowflakes as it moves. Behind it, forms, running –more soldiers. He can't discern well over Astra's head, but all he can see is black uniforms, long legs, and broad shoulders.

What the timers...?

"Did anyone lose a beast?" Karim's voice booms in the darkness, the mountains around echoing his words. 'Beast... beast... beast...'

Where did Karim's voice come from? And the white form... the beast? *Could it be...?*

"Ursa," Felix murmurs and the next second the huge, white bear is in front of his face, nostrils flaring, paws kicking up a storm of snow, as she runs at full speed and zooms past him, chasing the soldiers who are trying to run away towards the mountains. It's Ursa, she's here, he recognizes her nozzle, nostrils flaring in anger, her low growl, her white fur, glowing under the lights. She leaves a curtain of snow in her wake, the icicles slicing at his cheeks as he's left staring at her retreating back. She's the fiercest thing he's ever seen. How did she get here?

Felix feels something stir in his heart. Is it possible he's missed the sight of a merking beast so much? He and the Rebels are in the middle of being slaughtered over here, and all he can think about is how huge the bear looks as she's running clean through the enemy's lines, kicking up a storm of snow. How unexpected. How beautiful.

Karim's voice, wherever it came from, seems to infuriate her further, and she chases the soldiers away, into the darkness, her white skin glowing bluish in the radius of the lights from the Stadium above. Kun's soldiers are nowhere to be seen.

"Karim?" Felix yells.

"Yeah," a voice answers him and Karim materializes in front of him in full uniform, his eyes black and determined, his brow slightly shiny from sweat. Eight more soldiers from Felix's squad are there, next to him, staring at the bear's retreating form as she chases Kun's soldiers, eyes wide behind their goggles.

They came. They not only came; they came with the bear. *How in mars did that happen?*

"You're here," Felix observes stupidly.

"So what? So are you," Karim says, smirking. "Hey, did you *see* that? Is it one of the timer beasts they taught us about at school? I've never seen one up close, although-"

But Felix isn't listening. Waking from his shocked inertia, he turns around, to the rest of the cadets, yelling:

"Squad, fan out! Get into formation, as we trained, and dig your trenches. Two foxholes to my left, two to my right. Guns ready, do not open fire."

There are eight of Felix's cadets from the Academy, apart from Karim, filing in a line behind him. That's nine more than Felix expected to show. Karim's brought them. Malik is here, too, obeying him at once, falling to his knees, his hands working so quickly they're a blur. They've all trained for this, outside Ulysses' ice shack. He hadn't counted on the bear showing up to defend them, nor does he know where she came from, but while she's chasing Kun's soldiers around, maybe, just maybe, Felix's cadets and the Rebels will have enough time to get their act together.

They hunch down in the snow and start digging with their hands. They dig deep enough so that their bodies, laid flat or crouched inside the narrow trenches, will be covered completely, invisible to Kun's guards. Only the tops of their heads and their weapons will be raised above the brim of the trenches, so that they can take aim. After that... it's anyone's guess.

"Thank you," Felix gasps to Karim, who helps him dig a space around his and Astra's bodies, so that they're as invisible as the rest of them inside the snow trenches. He keeps a firm grip on her the entire time, scared that she'll slip into unconsciousness and he won't know to keep her breathing. "What changed your mind?"

"Remember when I followed you into the Pod, when I was four and you didn't give me away?"

Felix nods. That happened more than ten years ago, but he has never forgotten. They would have killed Karim that day, four years old or not.

"Well, that's why I came for you," Karim says. "The others are just idiots who followed me."

At least Karim hasn't lost his sense of humor. They might all lose their lives, but he'll go down calling everyone 'an idiot'.

"Ear comm.s?" Felix asks.

"We turned them off before going into the Pods."

Felix nods curtly.

The idea to dig foxholes came to him when he was playing 'forts' outside the shack with Astra, days ago, stars help him. But later, in the days Astra was gone, he actually trained his Squad to conceal themselves in the snow, to become one with it, each digging a small hole, lifting their guns just over their heads, eyes peering over the ice. Within minutes all that's visible is the flop of Felix's black hair. "How did you-?"

In the distance, a line of guards have escaped Ursa, and are running back towards them, looking in confusion around, seeing no one. There's utter darkness, further away, outside the circle of the Perennial light projectors. Felix's cadets are invisible.

"The timer beast followed us all the way from your shack," Karim replies in a quiet voice, not taking his eyes off Kun's guards. "Don't know how it found us again after that train ride. Then we hid out there, in these merking freezing plains, like you asked us to," he gestures to the dark plains ahead, "and the beast just sat there, watching us. But then the noise started and... it freaked out. Will you get your hands dirty, pretty boy?" he asks, flexing his muscles.

He keeps eyeing Astra with something like disgust in his expression. It irritates the merc out of Felix.

"I'm not leaving her," he says, tight-lipped.

"Put me down, you idiot," Astra says, having recovered the use of her voice. She's still shaking silently in his arms, though, her body rigid with pain.

"Don't tell me what to do," he tells her.

A bullet zooms past his ear. Merc. The guards are trying to figure out their position. Kash sends a torrent of bullets blindly into the guards' direction before he can hear Karim yell at him, over the noise, to stop wasting their ammo.

"Wait them out," Felix whispers calmly.

Kun's guards are firing blindly towards them; they don't have a clear view of their target yet and opening fire would just give Felix's men away. Instead, he's motioning to them to start taking down the guards, one shot at a time.

"Somebody has to tell you what to do," Astra says to him, and starts scrambling to get out of his arms. Immediately she goes limp with pain, stifling a scream.

"Ok, ok, I'm putting you down," Felix says quickly, moving to put an arm behind her back as he lowers her into the snow, behind the line of cadets. "If you feel like you're getting worse, you grab my leg and I'll know, all right?" A gun is thrust into his hand immediately.

"If I feel like I'm dying, you mean," Astra says, laying on her side and gathering her legs close to her chest as though she's trying to contain the pain.

He doesn't reply. He just checks that the Protector .44 Karim gave him is loaded, and moves on up after covering her with his cloak. His keeps his eyes fixed on hers until he gets into battle position. While Kun's men steadily advance towards them from the plains, the Rebels creep on the snow and kneel, starting to form a protective barricade in front of the cadets.

"Why the timers are you putting your hands all over an Island girl?" Karim asks him in a whisper as he takes his place beside him, lining up the next shot.

"Shut up," Felix says, as another bullet lands in front of his boot.

He takes aim and the next second a guard falls, wounded on the shoulder.

"What do you need?" Luke's voice asks behind him, and Felix quickly motions at him to get down. He lifts his head over the brim briefly: ten more Rebels are behind him -the rest must still be occupied inside, the hackers keeping the Dome down, the fighters blocking the exits. The rest are crawling on their hands and knees on the snow, uniting their forces with his squad, joining them silently.

The Rebel boy, recovered, is among them.

"Jonas!" Astra squeals in that croaky voice, as happy to see him, and the Rebel grabs her hand, bringing it to his lips without a word. Then he starts digging his own foxhole expertly, and lies down on his stomach in it. He still looks pale, his brow bathed in sweat, and Felix feels like he could punch him in the nose for some inexplicable reason.

"Make room, they're with us," Felix says to his cadets. "You don't have a gun, do you?" he asks Luke without turning to look at him.

"You'd be surprised," Luke replies and turns around to exchange a glance with the rest of the Rebels. In one collective motion, they each reach behind their backs and pull out half a dozen thin rods, buzzing with power from their belts. They stick them upright, in front of them in the snow.

"What are these?" one of the cadets asks.

Luke doesn't answer. He grabs a bendy thing that's strapped onto his back. It looks thin and dark and weightless. He stretches it in his hands, muscles bulging. Then he balances one of the thin rods between his fingers, takes aim, and lets it fly.

"Arrows," Malik says. "Arrows carrying voltage. Colonist-made."

"Quite," Luke replies. "Do you want your soldiers to kill the Chairman?"

"What?" Felix asks, surprised. "Oh. I don't know. Do I?"

Luke just sends him a look and Felix yells at the cadets that if they see a tall figure not to shoot at it because it's Chairman Kun. Although they probably won't even see him, because his guards will protect him.

Turns out his guards do protect him.

They are too many and they manage to advance, no matter how many bullets and arrows the Rebels and Felix's cadets shoot at them from the trenches.

The night air rings with shots, muffled cries and grunts as the Rebels and the cadets fight to stay alive. The snow is smeared with blood. The Chairman's guards and soldiers advance, until they're standing a few steps from the fringe of the trenches. Pretty soon it will be pointless for the

cadets and Rebels to remain down in their
foxholes, but until then the cadets preserve their
bullets, and shoot with precision, taking down
more than ten men. Some of the guards get up
after being shot, as though they're hardly human,
and keep walking. Felix bites down hard on his lip,
determined not to give the order to leave the fort
before it becomes absolutely necessary, ducking a
bullet that grazes his left cheek. And then, as
suddenly as it started, all noise stops.

The cadets cease fire as abruptly as if their arms
had been cut off with an invisible knife. The other
side stops shooting a split second later. Luke
freezes.

Felix's cadets stay immobile, hardly knowing
what to say, what to do. Their chests are puffing,
their brows sweating, their boots covered in icy
mud.

The snow the guards' steps have kicked up
settles back into the ground and, as it clears, two
rows of black-clad soldiers appear, their gun-
holding hands lowered at their sides. They've
reached the trenches, they're looking down at the
cadets.

But they're not moving.

Slowly, the cadets and the Rebels get to their
feet and climb out of the trenches, although no one
is holding them at gunpoint. He is the one who
announced their position to Kun's guards by
deliberately standing up. And that's not all he did.

"What are you *doing*?" Karim hisses to someone between horrified gasps.

"What does it look like?" Malik replies.

That's it. Him. *He* is the reason everyone's frozen.

Malik has turned his gun on Felix's head and is balancing it on his left temple.

Of course. He's turned traitor. It's over. Felix stays absolutely still. He shouldn't be surprised, not really. There never was much chance of them staying alive anyway. The only reason they've survived so far is the dugouts and fort thing, which, to be honest, he never really thought would actually work when he was training his cadets outside Ulysses' shack. Yet it did.

It did. The first thing he's done right. The only thing, perhaps. That, and pulling Astra out of the water. And kissing her, maybe, although that almost ended really badly. Stars, he's so tired.

Standing a few steps away from him, the soldiers part and the Chairman's silhouette advances between them.

"Why would...?" Karim starts asking, incredulous.

"Stop talking, Rim," Felix says calmly. "He's betrayed us."

That shuts him up fast. It shuts them all up. Malik doesn't speak, but he doesn't shoot either. His eyes are fixed on the Chairman's as he approaches, waiting for further instruction.

Complete silence descends as he holds Felix at gunpoint until Kun is standing right beside him.

Snowflakes keep drifting from the sky. The soldiers' hair is damp. Not that anyone has the time to notice such things.

Chairman Kun approaches his son.

Felix takes in his face, his light-colored hair that's cut close to his scalp, his height. He has those big, dark eyes that used to belong to the Asian race, but now belong to none, just to the people who happened to get this gene in the Elimination System lottery.

Of course Kun got them from his mother, probably, because Ulysses' eyes weren't turned up at the corners. Felix's own eyes are a bit rounder, but still they look almost identical to the Chairman's, only his are blue and Kun's the deepest black. He's the same height as the Chairman, and it's weird how their faces are on the same level, almost exactly alike.

Except of course, the Chairman's face doesn't have a gun pressed to its side.

In his father's eyes, Felix sees the sadness Ulysses spoke of, he sees the hunger and the need. He probably wouldn't have, if he hadn't been warned about them, because the Chairman's face is like the dark sky overhead: closed, blank, revealing nothing. One has to know where to look.

There's something else in there as well, something in the corners of his eyes as he fixes them on Felix's cadets, something that takes Felix by surprise. Ulysses didn't speak of it.

He looks tired. He looks as though he's given up. Is it because he knows the Commander of Venus is coming to obliterate them all anyway, no matter what happens? Or is it because his plan with the Virus failed? Whatever it is, it makes his face look horrible. Hollow and dark and... empty. His father's face.

I came from this man, Felix thinks. He feels nothing.

"What," Kun says slowly, and his well-known voice sounds even more imposing up close than coming from a PR's speakers, "did we talk about?"

He's speaking to Malik, not even glancing in Felix's direction. It's giving Felix the creeps.

Malik looks panicked.

Anger is boiling inside Felix's chest.

"S...sir?" Malik tries to say, but Kun is already speaking again.

"You're to shoot now," he says, as if he's talking to an imbecile. Malik turns slightly green, and his finger trembles near the trigger. He stops, right before pushing it. Felix ventures a sideways glance to see what's taking so long.

He comes face to face with Karim's shoulder. Oh, so that's why Malik is hesitating: Karim is pressing his own gun to Malik's head. Immediately the other three boys imitate him. Great.

Kun doesn't seem to have even noticed. "After you're done with him and the girl, take care of your fellow-officer traitors, would you?" he says, pretending to disregard the fact that if Malik even thinks of pressing the trigger, his 'fellow-officers' will blow his brains out.

Malik, though, doesn't disregard it. He regards it very much indeed.

In fact, he's frozen to the spot, and not the kind of freezing that has to do with the snowflakes landing on his cheeks and hair. The bad kind. Chairman Kun sighs loudly.

"We're not the traitors, father," Felix says, loud and clear, in a sudden inspiration. He's going to die anyway, why not go out with a bang? He's thinking quickly.

He may not have played Ulysses' entire Vis in the Dome, but right now, here, there are a few of the most prominent members of the Counsil as well as the Chairman's personal Guard in front of him, not to mention the Rebels and his cadets. Everyone's attention is focused on him.

What more could he want?

It doesn't sound like the cool and collected 'hello, father' he's been rehearsing below-stage, but it's somehow better. It sounds mature, as though the words are spoken by a man, not a boy.

"Constantine Hunter," Felix starts again, "in front of these witnesses, as your natural-born human son and the product of your Felony, according to the Counsil's laws, I demand that you step down from your position as leader of the One World and Chairman of its Counsil. I further accuse you of high treason. You are an enemy to the people of the Planet and to the One Peace you swore to protect with your life. You killed Christopher Steadfast, your brother," Felix continues in one breath, before he's interrupted, "in order to conceal your crimes against humanity and to proceed to commit greater ones."

"Last chance, Drone," Kun says to Malik, motioning one of his own guards to approach Felix, in case Malik fails to follow his order for a second time.

Drone, Felix thinks. The most insulting thing you can call someone in the One World. *He called him a merking 'Drone'. The man we've been serving and protecting our entire lives really thinks of his soldiers as Drones.*

His insides turn.

"You know this. But today I'll tell you something you don't know," Felix goes on in a steady voice, as though he's not a click away from dying. "I'll tell you that Steadfast died of his own will and that you didn't, you *couldn't* kill someone like him, or what he fought for, even if you tried. I didn't know him, but from what I do know, I think I'll consider his friends mine."

You could drop a match on the snow and it would echo in the silence. Everyone's eyes are glued to Felix. The gun stills at his temple. Malik is ashen, scared. His own life is threatened as well by Karim's gun. He can't shoot, but he can't move away either. What a mess.

"Christopher Steadfast," Felix says, lifting his hands in the air and splaying his fingers until the gun he was holding drops useless to the snow, "died for his friends; I won't die for my friends. I'll die for my enemy."

Kun doesn't say anything for once. His eyes have taken on a dark, dangerous look -still not looking at Felix- and Felix thinks that at least he's managed to get some sort of emotion in them. Not that he's sure that's a good thing.

s i x

"Drop your guns, soldiers," he says to his cadets. "That's an order." He has to repeat it, because they don't obey him at first. "Do it!" he yells.

Slowly they lower their arms - he sees them from the corner of his eye. All eight of them. Karim, too. Malik is standing alone, free to shoot him.

"*Dude*," Karim whispers. His voice sounds a bit wobbly, unsure. Felix would like nothing better right now than to turn to him and ask him whether he's going to cry like a baby, but he'd better keep his eyes fixed on the Chairman.

He wants to die staring him in the face.

"Proceed," the Chairman says to Malik, ignoring Felix, repeating the same thing he said inside the stadium.

Time to die, Felix thinks. *At least you made some noise. Silence is not peace. Remember the red of Astra's hair. Remember the blue of Steadfast's eyes. Remember the white of Karim's face as they made him a murderer.*

There are worse ways to die than beneath a velvet sky, snowflakes melting on your lips.

He never thought he'd see her again. Now he's dying, but she's right here. He's dying right next to her.

"Felix," Astra's voice murmurs from his feet.

"I hate to leave you, match girl," he whispers under his breath, thinking of the story they read about the tin soldier who became a flame. Who became ash. He refuses to allow his lips to tremble even slightly. "See you in the next match's flame."

"*Felix*," Astra says.

'The tin soldier, dressed in flames,' he thinks.

He's dying with the sound of his name on her lips.

tin soldier

Felix waits patiently for Malik to gather the courage to kill him in cold blood, but as the seconds slip by, his self-control is beginning to waver. *Don't make a fool of yourself in front of the match girl*, he chides himself. *Keep it together for one more second, for mars' sake.*

"Now," Kun says sweetly.

Malik presses the trigger.

"Felix!" Astra hisses the second before the shot zooms at him, and in that second he finally realizes what she's been trying to say to him.

She's not saying goodbye. She's telling him to duck.

So he does. Pain explodes near his eardrum, but he doesn't die. There's a thump on the snow as Malik falls on his ass, screaming in pain. His gun skids away from reach, and Felix reaches out and grabs it.

"Don't move, son," Luke says to Felix in a low voice. He's bending down, his face obscured, but Felix can see his arm muscles tense beneath his tunic as he's pressing one of his high-voltage arrows into Malik's leg, right at the spot where his boot ends and his Hydro suit begins. Malik keeps crying out in pain, but Luke doesn't let go.

The bullet just nicked Felix's ear. Blood is pouring freely from it, soaking his shirt, but it hardly hurts and the bleeding will stop soon. He feels the warmth of Karim's hand on his back and nods curtly. Still here. Still alive.

Felix can feel Karim's back coiling beside him, muscles readying for fight, but he doesn't turn his head a fraction of an inch. *This is your fight*, Karim's stance seems to say, *since you weren't killed and all.*

With an exasperated sigh, Kun lifts his gun and levels it between Felix's eyes.

Felix drops to the ground in a fluid, quick motion, without a second's hesitation. The cadets fall on the Chairman's guards and within seconds, it turns into a full-blown hand-to-hand combat. The cadets are pushing the guards' guns away with their bare hands, bringing their knees up to connect with the guards' foreheads, sending them flat on their backs. Of course, they're only six, including Felix, and even though the Rebels jump in to help, pretty soon they're surrounded on all sides.

A boy falls to the left, blood pouring from his forehead. Felix turns around and his eyes meet Karim's.

They exchange a glance.

Karim shrugs, then takes a forceful stride forward.

"No," the word rises to Felix's throat, but it's already too late.

Karim grabs a guard's arm, shifting the man's weight close to his chest, and presses his gun to his throat. Immediately the other guards freeze. It lasts only for a second or so, their immobility, but it's just enough for the cadets to see that the man Karim is holding hostage must be someone important: he's wearing the Chairman's insignia. In a moment, Felix recognizes him: he's a huge man, taller even than Felix. He was one of their training corporals in the Academy a few years ago. *Oh great.* The next instant, there are two to three guards to each of Felix's cadets, holding them at gunpoint. They're surrounded. *Merc.*

At least they hesitate before shooting, maybe because the Chairman is on his knees in the snow, a gash pouring blood from his temple where he was grazed by a bullet. Felix would bet anything he's never been forced to stay and fight in his life. He ran away when he was a kid and they were killing his mother; he sat safely in front of a PR screen as they were torturing Steadfast on that Caribbean island. Of course, he's one of the best soldiers this Planet has ever seen; in fact, his grades in the Academy had never been topped until Felix started training there. But his men have never seen him getting knocked off his feet or wounded and they are staring at him, uncertain. A few of them rush to help him to his feet.

"Agent one," Kun calls out, reaching out a hand to stop anyone from approaching him. He doesn't shout it in a commander's voice. He just pronounces the order calmly, rising to his feet gingerly, not even lifting his hand to shoot Felix. They got separated during the fight, and now there's a distance between them, but Felix knows that Kun wouldn't miss if he shot him. But he doesn't.

Immediately, another soldier takes Malik's place in front of Felix, leveling his gun between his eyes. Felix is once again powerless, threatened with a gun, which he has no doubt the guard will fire at him if he so much as moves.

Here we go again. How much longer is this circus going to last? This no-killing thing is bringing more trouble than even Astra did. Felix looks up, bored, to take a quick look at the guard holding him at gunpoint, lifting an eyebrow in contempt, but suddenly his eyes widen. He knows him. He was the star lieutenant of the Academy when Felix was first recruited as a cadet. His name is Burkhart, but they used to call him 'Puck'. Felix trained with him on several operations. He was kinder than anyone else he'd met in School back then -he's always remembered him like that. Right now he can't see his eyes, because he's wearing a pair of goggles just like the one Felix lost in the ice lake, but his lips are pressed tightly in a thin line.

Felix hasn't got a gun to drop this time. *Push the trigger already.*

Then something surprising happens.

Puck opens his lips and speaks. He doesn't lower the gun, he doesn't let him go, but he doesn't press the trigger either.

"What the old timer said in the Vis... Is it true?" he asks Felix.

Does he even remember me? Felix wonders.

"It is," he says in a clear voice, fixing him with a stare. "Every word."

"Then..." Puck doesn't get to finish.

His mouth drops open and his body jerks back as a red stain begins to blossom in the middle of his chest. Felix grabs his arm, trying to keep him from falling, but already his body feels too heavy in his hands, helpless. Dead.

Puck drops face-first on the snow, soundlessly, his body stiff like a rod, his pale face garishly lit by the Stadium flood lights. A trickle of blood drips from his mouth to stain the white ground.

Felix looks up. Kun is lowering his gun, a fierce look in his eyes. He's the one who shot Puck. He doesn't kill Felix, though, like he killed his own general. *What the stars is he doing?*

"Agent two," Kun says again, and now he's looking at another of his generals.

No one moves to approach Felix. Kun is waiting. And then realization hits Felix like a punch. *Oh. Oh no.* Kun won't kill Felix himself. Felix accused him of high treason, so it's Kun's soldiers who have to execute him. He wants *them* to do it. Maybe it's a test of loyalty or some other merking power-game thing like that. Three Counsil men, who used to be soldiers, and are now Kun's Generals, take a few steps closer to Felix. No one lifts a gun. *What's Kun going to do now?*

Is he going to start shooting them all in turn?

Felix's brain is on fire. Why did Puck hesitate? Why does every other soldier? Is it possible that they're starting to think? Is it happening already, right before his eyes?

He can't wrap his mind around it, a whole army waking up.

Kun sighs and lifts his gun. He actually sighs.

You're going to have to do it yourself, Felix thinks to his father, smiling to himself. *I've finally lost my mind, haven't I? What on mars am I smiling for?*

"Hey, Constantine!" he yells. "Looks like you'll have to do the dirty deed yourself."

His words jerk everyone out of their inertia really fast. The Chairman's guards snap to attention and lift their guns.

Stars take it, Felix thinks and starts moving. Kun is half a slope away, up there behind his soldiers' ranks, and Felix starts running towards him. *What's the worst that could happen? I die? That's gotten old by now.*

Immediately guns start exploding right and left, bullets chasing him, landing right at the heels of his boots, but his legs just keep pumping the snow, faster than the wind. The arctic air cuts through his suit like glass, and fresh snowflakes whip his cheeks. In the midst of all this death, he feels alive. As though the world has snapped into focus around him.

The smile spreads wider on his lips. He used to be a runner as a new recruit; he was the best in his year. He knows what he's doing. He doesn't run in a straight line, but dodges this way and that, going in an eight-shape up the slope, feinting to the left and right, as shots ring about his ears, zoom between his legs. One finds him on the left arm, right above the elbow, and he staggers as the searing pain slices his body like electricity.

The pain blinds him for a second and he doubles over, but his legs are still pumping the ground, still running in spite of the wound. He straightens up and keeps going, biting hard on his lip. *Come on, you can do this. Keep it together for a few seconds more, just keep your mind off the hurt, just-*

A roar sounds behind him, an ear-piercing cry so loud the mountains reverberate its echo, and the next second Karim is speeding past him, running even faster, bullets showering his suit's armor plates.

Not one finds his heart.

It's obvious that Kun's guards aren't aiming for it. What's not so obvious is why. Maybe they haven't decided yet who is telling the truth and who is lying. Maybe they've been forced to consider the possibility that Kun might be a murderer, a traitor. Felix hopes, for their sakes, that they'll make up their minds soon. He might not be around much longer, and this could very easily turn into just one tiny smudge in the Chairman's plans and nothing more, and his own existence forgotten before he's ever able to accomplish anything.

Then he can't think anything else, because Karim is barreling straight towards the Chairman. He's not running cautiously like Felix but madly, roaring a low, guttural sound and reaching out his hands in front of his chest, ready to grab him. Kun turns his body sideways sharply, as if to face him, and then lifts his arm, fist in line with his chin, aiming his gun straight at Felix's chest.

Felix's shoulder is beginning to go numb. It's darker up here, further away from the glowing Dome. Shadows are creeping towards him, the mountains looming in the distance. *Two more steps.*

Before Felix can even blink, let alone take two more steps, Karim, overtaking Felix, reaches Kun.

Unfazed by the guns trained on him, Karim slams into the Chairman bodily, at full force. Kun, staggering back a step or two, lunges for Felix, turning the gun on him, but right then, Karim plows into him like a bulldozer, making him lose his balance. Karim grabs Kun's hand, lifting it high above his head, the gun with it, and then he starts yelling. He screams and screams while wrestling the leader of the One World to the frozen ground, like he's one of his fellow cadets.

Felix sees the Chairman's left hand steal to his thigh and something gleams in the faint light. He's drawing out a knife.

Karim doesn't see it. He's too busy yelling in the Chairman's face, calling him a blood-thirsty Colonist Drone and a merking timer weasel-eater and a lot of other idiotic names, spit gathering at the corners of his lips.

"You'd have us executed just like that, your own soldiers, without even *asking* why we did what we did? You *killed* your own general!" he screams.

Felix reaches them, breathing heavily. The bullets have stopped coming, and all is silent for a second. Silent, except for the echo of Karim's words, ringing in the semi-darkness. Most of the soldiers are left behind them, in the lower plain. It feels as if they're alone. Karim just stands there, holding Kun, his nose practically touching the Chairman's, panting.

Felix, reaching him a second later, shakes his head at him, but Karim doesn't see him quickly enough. He doesn't see anything right now. It's understandable, his reaction; Karim's world is tumbling about his ears. *But, dude. Have a little dignity.* And then there's no more time for screaming and shaking of heads.

Kun brings his knife with force to Karim's stomach at the exact moment that Felix flings an arm in front of Karim's neck and pulls him back, shouting: "No, let me." And proceeds to punch his father full on the mouth.

Chairman Kun's head tilts backwards, a bright stream of red flowing from his nose, pooling on his lips. Felix feels him go limp against his body, and his eyes flicker closed for a second, but he's not out of it yet.

A slow smile spreads across the Chairman's face, his mouth red with blood, a front tooth hanging loose. For the first time he stares Felix straight in the eye.

"What are you fighting for, Drone?" he rasps. He struggles to free his fist, but Karim has both his arms in an iron grip, not letting him budge an inch. "They've already been infected in there," he says in a low voice, barely audible.

"I never released the virus," Felix hisses at him, "I threw it away, it's not even in the Clock."

Kun smirks. "The Dome *is* the Virus, silly boy." Felix feels the blood rush from his head. *What?* "I wouldn't rely on the stupid old timer for anything, I knew that. It was just a test, which both he and you failed spectacularly. If you'd care to take a look behind you, you'll see that the Dome is back up. The Virus is installed in its crystals, and it was released just as you and your Drones were foolishly opening fire on my Guard. Not that you'd understand the engineering that went into creating a structure of this caliber, my stupid mistake. You're as dumb as the rest of them. My Drones killed Ulysses instead of the little bitch, didn't they?"

"You mean Steadfast's daughter," Felix says, fuming. He's surprised Kun acknowledges him as his son so casually, *'my stupid mistake'*, when he was pretending he didn't even exist a second ago. Kun doesn't sound ashamed... just dismissive. And that fuels Felix's anger more. "They almost did kill her, but they hadn't counted on me." He doesn't even care that he called him 'his stupid mistake'. But calling Astra *that*... This deserves pain.

Felix punches him again, feeling Kun's jaw crack against his bones. It sounds as though Kun is chuckling as the blow lands on his face and his body falls back, his weight landing with a mighty thump to the snow. Felix stands over him for a second, knuckles bleeding, chest heaving, arm screaming in pain. He doesn't even care to look behind his shoulder, to check if anyone has a gun trained to his back. He doesn't even care.

'They've already been infected in there.' No. No, dammit, no.

"Luke, Karim, everyone all right?" he yells as he places a boot on either side of Kun's hips, trapping him on his back on the snow, helpless.

"Yes, sir, Lieutenant Hunter, sir!" Karim yells back, and for once his voice is dead serious.

"Didn't think you had it in you," Luke pants, as he runs up the slope and stands next to him, "Hunter."

"To be so quick on my feet?" Felix asks.

"To be so stupid," Luke replies.

Felix disagrees, but there's no point in standing here, at the top of the mountain, arguing about what's already done. Especially when his cadets are being held prisoners by the guards' guns. On the other hand, with Kun down, maybe his soldiers will let them go. Maybe it's worth just giving them the order to free themselves from the guards' hold; he wants to see what will happen.

"Squad, line up!" Felix calls to his cadets, before turning towards the closed gates of the Stadium.

Someone bumps into him from behind and he stumbles. The next second his arms are grasped roughly and brought behind his back with so much force it feels as though they'll be wrenched out of their sockets. "I arrest you in the name of the One World's peace," a guard's voice says in his ear.

Felix groans. Not again.

eight

"Told you it was a stupid idea," Luke snickers as he bends down and places a hand on Kun's shoulder, arrow at the ready in case he wakes up. Felix turns around, the guards' hands clasped firmly on his wrists. It's a different guard.

Luke is right there, kneeling above the fallen Chairman, and no soldier dares approach him for fear of what he might do, but he can't free Felix either. The rest of the Rebels are standing below, their bows stretched in their hands, aimed at the guards' heads. Matt and the rest of the hackers are among them. But all nine of Felix's cadets are restrained by Kun's guards, and the guards are not letting up, in spite of their leader having been knocked unconscious. There's no way the cadets can fall in formation or even move. It's over. Kun was right, the Dome is back up, looming in a fluorescent pale blue light behind their backs.

He lifts his eyes. No reinforcements are appearing yet from Kun's troops, which is surprising. The Rebel hackers may have messed with the Chairman's signal, but that would require the highest level of education and training. We're talking Elite and even higher than that. That's not possible, is it? Then again, there's a bigger problem: if the hackers even tried to tamper with the signal, they must have been inside the Dome's underbelly long enough to be infected with the other guests when the Virus was released. Or did they get out in time?

It's not over yet, it's not over yet, it's not over yet, Felix repeats to himself like a mantra as the seconds tick by to the rhythm of his heartbeat. No more than a few minutes passed while all of this has been happening, even though it feels like years. The people in there, the infected guests, they're just like Kai, the little boy in the Snow Queen story, trapped inside her ice palace. *I'll think of something. We'll think of something.*

Felix turns to the guard who's restraining him and, with no warning, he slams his knee as high as he can, into the guard's face, but the guard ducks just in time and pulls out his gun to press to Felix's head. Another guard, a giant of a man, is creeping silently up to Karim, but none of the others see him, since their attention is elsewhere. It's an impasse. The cadets are at a standstill with Kun's soldiers, locked in their positions, guns at the guards' throats, guns at their own. But as Kun's guards are starting to look uncertain, and Felix

"Rim!" Felix yells to Karim at the last moment, and Karim turns just in time to plant a punch on the giant's stomach, then whip out his gun. "Hold your fire," Felix says with as much authority as possible with a Slayer .34 pressed to his cheek. "Luke, I need the Dome to be sealed shut, no Pods, no door, no exits, nothing."

"You what?" Luke says. He hasn't heard Kun's words about the Stadium: they were whispered so quietly that no one heard but Felix.

"Now," Felix says, "That's an order." The next second Luke is yelling to Matt to get over there and seal the place tighter than the Box. "Two fighters and two hackers should go, the rest are needed here."

"I'll go. Stay in or out?" Matt answers from somewhere to his right.

Felix closes his eyes for a moment. It's almost certain that Matt has been infected as well, since he stayed behind with the others to keep the Dome down for as long as he could.

In a minute, the Elite and other guests are going to scramble for the Pods, then try to get on the train to escape to their homes. And that's the entire Planet infected. The Rebels crashed the system before getting out to fight, which is the only reason any of them are alive right now. But the system is up again and that opens up a whole world of merking possibilities.

Felix makes a swift decision. No one heard what Kun told him. The Rebels who are infected came into the fight late, plus they're out here in the open air. He's got to hope they haven't passed the virus on to others yet.

He's got to hope this isn't the end.

"Stay in," Felix says, knowing full well what that means. "Stay in, please, Matt." He remembers how the Rebel looked last night on the mountain, his eyes fierce, his hands smudged, calloused, strong. His cotton pants the color of the forest that was stretching below the steep cliff behind him. "Go, now!"

The Rebels start running immediately. Without Kun, his guards are just standing there, numb, uncertain. Their gun-brandishing hands waver. They're trained to take orders, to kill in battle, even in cold blood. But they're not trained to think on their feet. They've never been told what to do if everyone who is supposed to give them orders is out for the count. Their confusion is Felix's main weapon right now.

Felix is planning to use that to his full advantage before Kun wakes up, but he sees something from the corner of his eye and his blood freezes. Impulsively, he shifts his legs to start running, but at the last moment he realizes he can't move or the gun at his head will explode.

"Karim," Felix says, trying to sound calm, "I need you to get up and do something for me, will you?"

"I'm kinda..." Karim gasps. He's still struggling to contain this giant of a guard who's attacked him. Karim's fingers are pressing at the guard's throat on the snow, as they push against each other, each trying to surpass the other's strength. "...in the middle of something here."

But Felix doesn't even look over to him. His eyes are fixed somewhere across the plain, on Astra.

Her head is moving from side to side as though she's convulsing, her body shaking. Little grunts escape her, and she's brought her hand to her mouth, biting her fingers in order to stop herself from screaming. Already her movements are getting weaker.

A few paces away, Malik is still lying on his side, unconscious.

The hurt Rebel, Jonas, follows Felix's gaze to Astra's body in the trenches and the next moment he's running to her, limping, his bow at the ready. He reaches her and slides to his knees on the snow, placing a hand on either side of her head, trying to keep it still.

"Hey," Jonas whispers to her, cupping her cheek. "Astra, hey, I'm here, you're safe. You'll be fine, ok? Just breathe." He rolls her to her side, supporting her back.

Felix swallows, turning away. He can't stand to watch her hurt so badly. He feels physically sick, as though he was the one suffering. The familiar pain starts to throb in his chest again, choking him. He tries to swallow past it, his Adam's apple bobbing, a muscle ticking on his jaw.

"One of you take Karim's place," Felix says to his other two cadets, and the guard holding him at gunpoint tries to place his hand across his mouth to silence him, but Felix bites down hard and continues speaking as soon as the guard's withdrawn it with a yelp. "Release Karim, he's got something to do for me." His voice sounds hoarse, stars take it. He tries to clear it discreetly, without sounding like a total wimp.

Jonas is bending his head next to Astra's. "Hunter," he calls, his voice frantic, carrying across the distance. Felix tries to free himself with a jerking movement, but he's pulled back roughly by the guard. His eyes are stinging. *Dammit, match girl, I told you to hang on.*

He nods to Kash, who escapes easily from the confused guards and walks over to take Karim's place, lacing his fingers around the giant guard's throat. Felix knows Kash is solid, maybe stronger than Karim, but he's even younger and his eyes look panicked, fierce in his dark face; he's out of control. The remaining guards tense, begin to raise their weapons again. If they see Kash kill the guard, they'll open fire, without an order, Felix is sure of it.

"Careful," Felix tells Kash as calmly as he can. "Look at me. *Look* at me." Grunting and gasping, Kash does. In a second, his eyes reflect the calmness of Felix's gaze. "Good. Don't suffocate him, ok? Just knock him out."

Kash squeezes the giant's neck, then stands back up. "Done," he says.

"Pfft," Karim says.

"Rim, I need you to take one of the Discs in your suit and go slip it between Astra's lips," Felix tells him.

Beside him, Luke doesn't take his eyes off Astra's still form. He stifles a curse, looking just about ready to drop Kun and go do it himself.

"I'm not touching her," Karim says at the same time that Astra's voice, faint and choked, but still as annoying as ever, says:

"I'm not swallowing that."

Luke lets out a snort that's half laughter half sob. Felix would like nothing better than to walk over there and strangle both the match girl and his cadet, but he can't even move, or he'll die. He's trying to ignore Jonas' fingers on her cheek, his knees braced next to her back, his strong hands holding her upright. All he cares is about is that the Rebel is keeping her alive.

"You'll have to help her," he calls to Karim, trying to keep himself from screaming, "Hold her head, or she'll choke. Hurry, Karim. She's... she's dying." The words come out with difficulty, but they do -that's all that matters. No time right now to feel weak for crying in front of his cadets and the Jonas kid.

"Well, look around you. Who isn't?" Karim retorts, but his voice sounds gruff.

He runs down the slope to Astra and kneels next to her head. He and Jonas exchange a few quiet words that don't quite reach Felix, and in a second he hears a gurgling cough coming from her.

"It's done," Karim says.

Astra keeps coughing, and Felix shuts his eyes tight. "Swallow it, match girl, come on," he murmurs.

"Yes, swallow it," a well-known voice repeats to his left. "Get well soon, Steadfast girl, so that you'll fry like your coward of a father. There's more where that came from."

Kun's awake.

nine

Before Felix -or anyone else- has time to react to Kun's words, there's a click. The giant has come to and broken free from Kash's hold, already up and running towards Astra, gun pointing her chest. His eyes shift from his aim to somewhere to his left, and Felix follows his gaze. Kun is awake, but not standing yet.

The Chairman half-raises himself from the ground, gritting his teeth, and turns his battered face towards the tall guard. "Delta 2," he calls in his commander's voice, " the girl. Make the shot."

Delta 2, that's the tall, giant-looking guard, is now about two hundred meters away from Astra's body. He freezes in his tracks and fixes her with his eyes.

"Astra!" a frantic, shattered voice yells. It takes Felix a second to realize it's his own voice. His knees turn to water.

Delta 2 pulls the trigger. Felix's heartbeat pound in his eardrums.

A gunshot rings in the silence. A faint scream.

A thud.

Astra's voice calling Jonas' name hoarsely, catching on a sob. Two Rebels barreling towards his fallen, still form, the others covering for them, all of them moving quickly, soundlessly, so fast they're almost a blur. Then Karim is on his feet, turning towards the giant, Delta 2, and burying his Slayer .34 in his stomach. He hesitates for a split second before pulling the trigger, then he raises it to his shoulder and shoots to wound, not kill. Kun doesn't order his soldiers to attack anyone else.

Delta 2 moans, but he doesn't fall. It takes a solid kick by Karim's boot in his chest to bring him with a thud to the ground. Felix turns around, despite the gun on his temple, to stare murderously at Luke, who's pushing the arrow into Kun's leg. "Push it in!" he screams. "Further. What are you doing? Luke!"

That was Luke's only job, to keep him unconscious. Why is Kun even awake? He shouldn't be, not with that arrow sizzling with voltage entering his bloodstream. Felix is struggling to get his hands free, turning his shoulders violently this way and that, trying to escape, but there are two soldiers restraining him now, one on each side, keeping him immobile, trapped. At least, not dead. For now.

From somewhere behind him, Luke lets out a frustrated grunt, pressing his arrow deeper into Kun's thigh. Felix stifles a curse. *What on mars is up with Luke?* Why isn't the Chairman screaming in pain by now? Any human being would be fried, possibly dead, if they had that high voltage arrow

pressed into their veins for so long. But Kun isn't
fazed by the arrow cutting into his skin, buzzing
with electricity. At all. The arrow is powerless
against him. And so is Luke.

Down in the valley, by the Dome, Jonas' body is
lying on top of Astra's, a hole gaping on his back,
where the guard's shot found him. He took the
bullet instead of her. Felix gulps, he can't breathe.
*This isn't happening. It's not real; it's a
nightmare.* He'll wake up any minute now, and the
few men who took a chance on him, the few men
he swore to protect will all be safe and alive.

But they aren't. Jonas is not breathing, Felix
can see that from all the way up there; he can see
from the way he just lays there, not moving.
Astra's face looks paler than the snow as she tries
to sit up, her eyes wide, unseeing. She's trying to
raise him off her, but her arms won't obey her.

Felix feels a sadness cover him like a wave, a
sadness so profound that he wants to lie down in
the snow and sleep. *It should have been me*, the
thought pops in his head out of nowhere. *It should
have been me that saved her, it should have been
me who died. My life is worth nothing, not
compared to them. That bullet was mine.*

But it's still not over. Kun, raised to his knees
now, is staring right into Felix's eyes as he lifts his
gun in Astra's direction. His hand is shaking
slightly, but his eyes are steady and fierce and
Felix doesn't doubt for a second he can hit her,

even from up here. Kun's nose is swollen with dried blood, his jaw turning purple. He's on his knees in the snow, and the tip of Luke's arrow is pressing against his leg, sinking into his skin, but the voltage doesn't seem to bother him as much as it should. Luke's eyes are wide, but whether from panic or from the effort of pushing in the arrow, Felix isn't sure.

"Killing the coward Steadfast's girl," Kun says, panting, "is taking so much longer than it should have." He raises his voice so that it carries all the way down the slope. "Any volunteers to kill the most wanted criminal of the One World?"

There's an ugly, blood-smeared grin plastered across his cheeks. He's not even bothering with Luke, next to him. He's only focused on Astra. On killing her. He wants her to hear him before she dies. He wants her to hear him call her father a coward.

"Luke, come *on!*" Felix says, as another soldier starts marching over to Astra and Jonas' prone bodies, gun outstretched. "Knock him out."

"I'm trying..." Luke starts saying, panting heavily. Kun starts to get up, and Luke stops talking, struggling to constrain him, but for some reason, he can't.

Why won't anyone do what they're supposed to? Why won't anyone-? Felix pries his eyes away from the soldier pointing a gun to his head, sensing a sudden change around him.

During the few minutes it took Karim to give the Health Disc to Astra, the Rebels had slowly moved closer to her, and now they stand in a cluster around her, their elbows touching, guns facing Kun's guards; they're shielding her with their bodies. They send a shower of arrows into the guards' uniforms. In response, a few of them open fire again. Kun is helped down the slope, inching his way to Astra, and Karim jumps to his feet and takes his gun out, but doesn't look too eager to pull the trigger. He's probably down to his last bullet. The fighting starts again.

Will this never end? Felix thinks helplessly. It's like a nightmare that goes on forever. Another one of the guards falls, dragging his injured leg behind him. One of the Rebels lets out a cry, but still keeps shooting arrows, blood streaming from his right thigh. *Is this what I've started? Is this what war actually is?* There's nothing heroic or strategic about it. Just people falling in the snow. Just people causing them to fall. Murderers and corpses. There are more bodies strewn about the mountain than he can count at a single glance.

And Felix is standing there on top of the hill helpless, watching it all, a prisoner. He's seriously considering risking a bullet to the head to charge into the battle, in spite of the guards' guns by his side. He takes a deep breath...

And then.

And then it stops. The guns, the fighting, the screams. All of it, it just stops.

No, it doesn't stop. *Someone* stops it.

Suddenly there's a flash of movement, and the next minute Chairman Kun starts making choking noises. His guards, scattered all around the plains, start yelling at each other, but there's pretty much nothing they can do, because they're obstructed by the Rebels and the cadets.

Felix looks down, towards the Dome. *Ah, merc.* Someone finally did what he wanted them to do. Only it's the wrong someone.

There's a reason why Kun is making these noises: Astra is crawling on her hands and knees, her braid a flaming red against the bluish-white glow of the snow, to reach the Chairman from behind. Kun is five paces away from her, momentarily distracted by a shower of bullets one of the cadets is sending in his direction. He dodges out of the way, and Astra leaps at the opportunity to sneak up on him.

Felix acts so quickly, he doesn't have time to think about the guns trained on him.

"Kash!" He screams at the top of his lungs. The guard on his left pushes the cold barrel of his Slayer .34 into the hollow of Felix's cheek. Felix tries to ignore it. "Kash!" It ends up sounding like a screech, his desperation palpable in his voice. It sounds as if he's speaking with his mouth full, because of the gun, but Kash hears.

The boy's eyes meet his across the distance. Felix nods, shutting his eyes. Kash, to his credit, doesn't hesitate once. He shoots the guard on Felix's right, who falls, thankfully before he can kill Felix, and immediately Felix packs a punch to the other guards' stomach. He's past caring about whether they'll shoot him dead. He starts running.

In the valley below, Astra reaches Kun from behind, and goes for his throat. Felix runs fast, but he can already see her small hands circling the Chairman's throat with surprising strength. Enough strength that he's choking. His heart in his mouth, Felix runs even faster, dodging bullets, gritting his teeth. The snow is slippery beneath his boots, and he abandons himself to the wind, only thinking of reaching her.

As he half-runs, half-slides down the mountain slope, Felix doesn't pay any attention to the guns aimed at him or the bullets grazing his skin. He keeps his eyes trained on Astra. She's still shaking and her skin looks ashen, but her eyes are flashing, and she's not coughing anymore. The pill worked pretty fast. She's just strong enough and Kun is just weak enough for them to be locked in the stupidest, deadliest, craziest idea the match girl's ever had. When he's halfway down, he bends and picks up a gun from a dead guard, cocking it. He can hear Astra's voice clearer with every step he takes; she's talking to Kun. He can also hear soldiers running behind to him, but right before they grab him, the Rebels shoot them down.

He's almost there now. Astra is not letting Kun go; she leans down and opens her lips.

"My father was *not* a coward," she spits into Kun's face, her voice sounding a bit hoarse, but steady. "You know what a coward is? It's someone who shoots a wounded girl in cold blood. It's someone who pushes a rod into his brother's neck. It's someone who puts a hole in the chest of just a boy, a boy who has more courage in his little finger than..." Her voice breaks.

Felix can see the teardrops drying on her cheeks, frosting her eyelashes as they freeze on her skin. Her shoulders are shaking with sobs, as though she's breaking inside. He reaches them, skidding to a halt on the snow, the glaring Dome lights blinding him. He doesn't dare get any closer because he can already see guns trained on her, although Kun's soldiers hold their fire for fear they will wound him as well. For the first time, he sees her expression clearly: she looks as if her heart is being torn to pieces, bleeding dry. And he can't do a damn thing.

"They say you're not stupid," Astra continues, and the Chairman's eyes bulge out of their sockets as she presses her fingers tighter, "although I see no evidence of your intelligence right now. Even so, you of all creatures should know what a coward is."

Felix thinks of all the times he thought she was mad at him; of all the times he thought *he* was mad at Kun, at the Clockmaster, at the world. Well, if he thought he's ever seen mad before, he was wrong. *This* is mad. This is years and years of knowing the truth and being forced to swim in a sea of lies and to learn to live with the pain and the loss and to survive against the tide of evil that's trying to drown you. This is never giving up, never getting too tired, no matter how many times they've killed you; always getting back up on bleeding feet and getting on with the battle. And becoming an amazing human being in the process.

It's all coming out of her now. She's like a force of nature: unstoppable.

"By the way, none of lieutenant Hunter's soldiers are Drones, you bastard," she goes on, her nose an inch from his. "Why would they have come here to fight you if they were? And speaking of brainless bastards, it's really smart what you do, calling the soldiers *you* created names. Killing them. Look at you now, ready to die at the hands of the daughter of the man who shamed you."

The Health Disc Karim gave her can't have fixed everything that's wrong with her body so soon, of course. She must still be in so much pain, but to look at her one couldn't tell.

"You don't know what you're doing, Steadfast," Kun gasps against Astra's fingers and Felix can just about catch the words. "If what's going to come out of the Stadium doesn't kill us, the Venus army will. Either way we'll all be dead in a couple of months. You can't even begin to imagine what their armies are capable of. This Planet is done."

"Oh, I don't know," Astra tells him. "We defeated you and your Drones. Look around you. Where are the rest of your guards? Your Venus reinforcements?"

Kun smiles that ugly, bloody smile. "Inside," he says. "Like your hackers."

Felix clenches his jaw. *'Like your hackers'. Infected, he means.*

Astra shrugs. "We'll take our chances."

Felix has to bite his tongue so that he won't scream at her to shut the merc up. But she trusted him with the Rebel camp coordinates. She trusted him with the life of her friends, including her own. He might as well do her the same courtesy.

"Will you now," Kun says, his voice dripping with contempt. "Or are you just planning for your Drone lover to take over my position?"

Felix sees it suddenly: Kun's arm stealing around Astra's waist, as she's sort of straddling him on the snow, yelling at him, and the blade of a small, silver knife he's got in his palm is sliding against the fabric of her shirt. Felix opens his mouth to warn her, but a beefy palm is thrust on his lips, choking him. He bites down, hard, trying to free himself.

"Felix," Astra says to Kun, her voice low and dangerous, "Felix is his name. *Your son's* name. You don't even deserve to pronounce it. And look, your soldiers already trust him more than you. Not that he'll ever dream of taking your-" Astra stops talking abruptly. Her cheeks don't look so pale and she isn't trembling in pain anymore, but she isn't moving a muscle either. Her hands go slack around the Chairman's neck.

She takes a sharp breath and Felix's eyes, frantic over the guard's palm, see the fabric of her shirt slice in slow motion, revealing the skin on her back underneath. It's turning dark with blood. A muffled sound escapes him, as he kicks at the guard, turning his gun around to shoot him.

His heart is beating like crazy, his chest is rising and falling rapidly. The guard's hand falls away finally, but it's no use, Felix can't do anything now. If he speaks, Kun will finish her. His hands are literally tied. *Luke, do something*, he thinks frantically, but Luke is just looking at him with wide eyes, his face a blank mask. He's got an arrow slung across his bow, but he isn't shooting it. What's the point? He had it pressed into Kun's leg's muscle before, and Kun didn't appear to be feeling any pain. It doesn't affect him. Who knows what he's done to himself to be immune to the tortures he inflicts on others?

That's when Felix realizes it. *Oh, stars.* Kun has taken the coward's way out: he's been sending his soldiers to fight a war he's immune to. Then again, hasn't that been the path the Chairman always walked on? A coward's path. And he's led the entire Planet on it. But that doesn't matter right now.

What matters is how helpless they all are to do anything to stop the murder happening silently in front of their eyes.

"You can't kill him again," Astra's voice says, sounding steady and sure, in spite of the knife slicing her skin. And a little bit sad, perhaps, which cuts Felix worse than if she were crying and screaming and begging to live. But of course she's never acted like a normal person before in her life, she's not about to start now. "Your brother. You can't bring him back, either. You did what you did to him and you have to live with it. Or you can humble yourself and admit you were wrong. There's still a chance, there always will be, as long as you're alive. But every time you destroy someone it gets that much tinier."

"You really are your father's daughter," Kun says, his voice for once sounding hoarse, as though his cool exterior is slipping. "Mouthing off when you're about to die. Pity."

"Pity for you, Con," a voice retorts from somewhere above them. "She's not only her father's daughter, you know." The voice pauses. "Or maybe you don't. You always pretended to be smarter than you actually are. She's her mother's too."

It's a woman's voice.

ten

Astra's head is spinning.

She didn't want to put another of those poisonous Health Discs inside her, but she could tell that her tin soldier was about to crumble to pieces, up on the hill, so she let the huge, dark-skinned boy put his hands on her face and slip the pill into her mouth.

Felix's friend didn't look too happy about it either, but he did it. But she can see why people took to the Health Discs. Not that they had any choice, of course, but it's just a few minutes later and the pain that was tearing her body apart is receding.

Now, she's back on the snow again; she was choking Kun with her bare hands mere seconds ago. And, despite her father's murderer's face staring her in the eye, she's feeling much better.

Or she was, until the murderer slid a knife into her back.

"She's not only her father's daughter, you know. Or maybe you don't. You always pretended to be smarter than you actually are. She's her mother's too."

And then this. A woman's voice slices the thick night. *Who the stars is she?* Astra balances her weight on her elbows and tries to stand up, only to feel the Chairman's knife slice further into her flesh. She stifles a gasp, and stays absolutely still. The knife stops, too. So he wants her silent and at his mercy, but not dead. He wants her alive.

And so she stays alive, for now, her mind racing with questions. She lifts her eyes to the mountains. Above the Dome, the dark sky explodes into a million shooting stars.

Her mind flies back to a few hours ago -it feels like days, but it was less than three hours ago. The beginning of the Perennial Celebration.

She was huddled in a corner underneath the stage of the stadium as per Luke's instructions, when she saw Felix for the first time after having left him four days ago. Matt was hunkered down beside her, passing his fingers over the screens expertly; he had the system hacked within seconds, changing the position of the Dome's panels and locking up every exit and Pod he could. Changing the Stadium's coordinates so that the reinforcements would miss the Pods by thousands of miles.

And then Perennial the guards let Felix in, explaining to him how he'd be lifted on stage and where he should stand.

She never knew she could feel like this. She thought she knew all there was to know about human closeness, having grown up away from the sterilized environment of Kun's minions, but she had no idea. She had no idea she could ever feel so close to someone, this nearness, this... oneness. She felt as if she could climb out of her skin and crawl into his. It wasn't just their lips that met, it was everything: their hands, their bodies, their breaths. She could feel his heartbeat as if it was her own.

She relives it now, for a delicious second, sigh for sigh, touch for touch, although she still feels strange simply remembering the things her lips did. Her hands, her body. Her... insides.

Not to mention her heart.

There was no sign of a nightmare this time, nothing like the terrors that wake her at night, leftover memories from her time in the Box. No sign of evil memories haunting her, dragging her down into the abyss. Everything else, everything that came before him, was forgotten in an instant.

How stupid to think she'd ever been kissed before... Those slimy fingers of a guard reaching for her, haunting her every night inside the Box... That had been no kiss. It had been a crime. *This* was real. This was fire.

'*She's the match*,' she'd overheard Felix say last night at the Rebel camp.

And so she was. So she is.

He turned her into a timer fire, the tin soldier - one of the roaring ones that used to consume everything that came near them, be it wood, paper or metal.

She heard his heart beat, too. She felt it beat against her skin while he was holding her. Wild, erratic, fierce. Human.

She realized at once what he'd done. The idiot attached his own heartbeat to the Clock. He put his Felony out on display for everyone to see. She'd be impressed, if she wasn't worried sick for him.

When the guard with the rod had reached for him, she didn't even have to think about it.

She'd stepped in front of him in a flash. There had been no hesitation, no thought, no choice necessary. *They're killing me the same way they killed father*, had been her last thought before the pain slammed into her neck.

Everything after that is a blur. She just remembers listening to Felix's heart try to find its rhythm against her ear, then lying on the cold, familiar embrace of the snow.

Opening her eyes to find Felix held at gunpoint, near death.

Jonas taking the bullet that was headed for her heart, then the heavy thud of his body on the ground, on top of hers. The slow, cold realization that Kun had killed her childhood friend. Kun's orders to kill Felix again, again and again.

Thinking, *don't look. As long as you don't look at him, he's still alive. Jonas. Jonas. I don't deserve your sacrifice.* And still looking, searching for a sign of life, but already feeling the weight of his absence, the hole of his loss.

Kun's guards. Kun's words. Kun's blade on her skin.

The gaping wound inside her that steals her breath but will not kill her, at least not directly, because the pain is sadness, not injury.

Then the voice, out of nowhere:

"She's her mother's, too."

eleven

"Luke," Astra turns to the Rebel, looking away from Kun's pathetic, bloodied face. "Have you any idea what-?" The blade makes her skin scream in pain, but what else is new.

But Luke is already on his feet, the Chairman forgotten, his eyes fixed somewhere above her head. "You always knew how to pick your moment," he says to someone through slightly trembling lips. His eyes are glowing strangely and his entire face is transformed. She's not sure if it's sheer joy or terror.

Astra can't turn around to see who he's talking to. Out of the corner of her eye, she sees figures walking towards them, silhouetted against the black sky as they're climbing down the mountain slope. Reinforcements. And they're Rebels -she would have known. Which part of the One World have they transferred here from? Maybe they're not even from Earth.

As they approach, she can see that there's a lone figure walking a few steps in front of the others. Slender and of medium height, the figure is dressed in the Colonist military uniform, which is made of rubber and elastic metal, and covers the entire body from neck to toe in a glistening silver, skin-tight material, melded to the skin. So that doesn't tell her anything, but the voice that spoke was very much a woman's, so Astra concludes that the 'she' Luke is referring to is the figure.

A single file of soldiers is marching in formation behind her.

"Who is she?" Felix asks, inching away from the guard who was restraining him, since said guard's eyes have grown huge as satellites, staring at the woman and the marching company behind her.

"She's who she says she is," Luke replies.

"Astra's... mother?" Felix says, pronouncing the word carefully as though it's liable to explode in his face.

"And then some," Luke says.

"What is that supposed to mea-" Felix begins to reply, but abruptly the voice dies in his throat. He looks at her and his face takes on the sickly, white color of utter horror.

At the same moment, she feels a sudden, sharp pain pierce her neck.

Kun's knife. He's pressing it against her throat, but he's not pushing it in yet. *Why doesn't he kill me already?* Astra's brain is starting to go dull with pain. *Why doesn't he-?*

"Steadfast," Kun whispers into her ear. His breath is raspy and so close, it blows little wisps of hair away from her clammy skin. He's practically on top of her, his weight pushing her into the snow. "Kill me."

Did he say what she thinks he said?

"Kill me," he repeats. "Do it, before *she* gets here. Kill me with my knife. Pretend to grab for it, I'll let you take it."

Before Astra can so much as open her lips to ask him what the merc he's talking about, he starts talking again, but in a different voice. It's loud and assertive; his Commander's voice.

And he's addressing the woman now: "Move," he says calmly, "and I'll end her."

"Don't think so," Felix's voice, warm and near, replies. Kun, in a sudden burst of anger, lifts his hand and brings the knife with force to her neck.

Instantly hands grab at her waist, *Felix's* hands, wrenching her away from the knife, crushing her to a beating heart. He's here, he's somehow escaped the guard who was holding him prisoner with his gun and he's shielding her with his body.

She gasps, letting out a relieved breath.

"All right," Felix breathes into her hair. "You're all right."

"Hands off, Hunter," the woman's voice says, sounding as though she's much closer now, and for a second Astra thinks she's talking to Felix. But she's not.

The Chairman has gotten slowly to his feet, and now starts circling Astra and Felix like a bird of prey. He's a bit unsteady on his feet, but his eyes are focused and dangerously calm, his arms poised for fight, knife at the ready, blood dripping from his nose. Felix begins to move as well, keeping his body between Kun and Astra, but Kun lunges with his knife between them and manages to take a swipe at her upper left arm, releasing a bright red ribbon of blood that flows all the way down to her fingers. The cut doesn't do much more than sting slightly, but even that seems to infuriate Felix so much that he shoves her back, almost sending her to her knees but not quite, and throws himself on the Chairman's neck.

Kun parts his bloodied lips and lunges. The Chairman doesn't have a reputation for being the fiercest warrior on the Planet for no reason. Limber as a cat, he leaps on top of Felix, who was already looking a bit white around the lips, probably from the nasty wound on his arm. Now he stumbles under the Chairman's weight, falling flat on his chest. At once he has one knee up, boot braced firmly on the ground. He punches Kun's stomach with his hurt arm, and Kun doubles over.

Astra's heart constricts at the sight of them tangled together, father and son, enemies. Worse than enemies, strangers. The night air is filled with their grunts and gasps as knuckles meet bone, knees collide with flesh.

Felix sweeps his left leg behind the Chairman's ankles and Kun's long body hits the ground as he falls hard on his back in the snow. Felix slams his bent knees into his opponent's stomach and the Chairman bashes his forehead against Felix's nose. They struggle on the ground for a couple of seconds, sending snowflakes spraying in an arch around them with every muffled grunt, until Felix finds an opening and leaps on top of the Chairman, locking his bent elbow around his neck.

Kun's face starts turning purple, but he doesn't struggle or protest.

"Kill me, then, Drone," he mutters.

The hairs on the back of Astra's neck stand out. The exact same words Kun said to her a few minutes ago. What is he playing at?

She's watching Felix's eyes. At the moment his blue irises look so dark in the dim light, they're almost black.

"Just admit that you're my father," he says to the Chairman in a low voice, panting, "and I'll let you go."

Kun is silent.

"You're wasting your breath," the woman's voice says. She's right next to Astra now. Her voice sounds fierce, but she keeps her voice low, as though she's used to giving orders. "He won't budge an inch. Although I have to hand it to you, for Con's son, you almost acted with courage there for a second. Saved my star's life. I owe you for that; you'll live." She nods towards her soldiers. "Platoon, advance."

And just like that, her soldiers move forward and flank the Chairman's men, even though Kun's guards have them outnumbered. Still, they have them under control and disarmed in less than two minutes. They stop longer by the officials, recognizable by Kun's insignia, and snap a pair of round metal bars between their wrists and ankles. The Chairman's guards surrender to the Colonist detail with almost no protest, and Astra, to her shock, sees that not even Kun is fighting back. He just stays where he is, passively watching everything that's happening. His soldiers look intimidated, unsure of themselves, stealing glances to their Commander, but before anyone can even blink, the Colonist soldiers have reached Kun. They free him from Felix's grasp and haul him to his feet, clasp the bars around his ankles and hands. Then they just stand next to him, waiting for the woman to approach him.

"What the timers do you think you're doing, Con?" the woman says. Her small, almost girlish figure is absolutely still as she faces the Chairman. The wind ruffles her short, silver-painted hair, but her eyes look mature, older. This is the second time she's addressed the Chairman by his real name.

Only the back of her head is visible to Astra right now, but judging from the Chairman's expression, she can imagine she's looking fiercely into his eyes. "Christopher's been gone for less than two years and already you're bringing the world crashing down about your ears."

Her tone is condescending, as though she's speaking to a child.

The Chairman refuses to meet her stare.

"I've been looking for a way to stop you for years," the woman continues. "You know that, of course. The entire Opposition, we've all been waiting for this day. And to think, it was your own son that brought it about! Thanks to the Vis recording of the Perennial... proceedings," she glances towards Felix, "well, thanks to Ulysses really, we finally have proof of your treason."

'We.' And she knows Ulysses' name. *Who the stars is she?* Astra wonders for the hundredth time. Why did she say '*we*'ve been waiting for this day'? Is she...? No, she can't be part of the Rebels. That's impossible. She's from another Planet, for mars' sake.

The woman lifts her head to the skies. The black sky is filled with stars, raining down over the mountain peaks like a shower of gold. "See those pretty stars in the sky?" she says to Kun, her lips curling in a disapproving grimace. "They're no stars, worm. They're my fleets, destroying the traitors' reinforcements coming to help you ruin your Planet. Since Ulysses exposed the truth, I was free to stop them."

Astra's blood runs cold. Is this true? Does she mean that she obliterated a whole army, up in the skies? *That starry rain was, in fact... Kun's reinforcements, shuttles coming to take over Earth. And this woman simply finished them off. She just said, with an indifferent flick of her wrist, that her fleets shot them down.* Astra can't wrap her mind around it. Such unfathomable power. Such a crucial choice. And all of it done in cold blood.

The Chairman looks up, too, but he doesn't seem surprised. Neither by what he sees in the skies, nor by what the Commander tells him. It's as if he was expecting it.

"This is no longer your Planet," the woman tells him. "You're done."

Kun just grunts.

"Nicely said," she says. "Also, last words." She turns to her soldiers. "Let's wrap this up."

One of the soldiers kneels down and adjusts the clasp of the brace on Kun's wrists. Uttering a piercing cry, he goes limp. Two other Colonist soldiers approach him, and support his weight between them. His eyelids flutter. He's still conscious, but he can't resist; maybe he's in pain, too. That must be what they did to him through the cuffs. Did they flood his bloodstream with an essence to make him submissive? Another Disc? They start dragging him towards the train tracks, up the hill.

If the woman is indeed a Colonist, then they're headed for the Intergalactic Station, a few minutes' ride from the Perennial Site.

But that's not the most incredible thing out of everything that's happened the last few minutes. All this time, while the military woman was descending the mountain and Felix and the Chairman were wrestling on the snow, not one of the remaining Rebels, the cadets or the guards made a move to interfere. At first Astra thought that it was because half of them were locked at a standstill, weapons pressed to their sides and throats from either side, and the rest were dumbfounded by the Colonist platoon filing down the slope.

But right now, she realizes something else.

Everyone -everyone but her- knew how this was going to end as soon as the woman's voice sounded.

And that's why they stopped resisting as soon as they saw her. Even the Rebels gave up. Even Felix's cadets relaxed their holds on their enemies. Seriously, *who the stars is she?*

The soldiers carrying Kun's limp figure away pause their progress to exchange a few words with the woman, turning their faces towards the light, and that's when Astra gets a clear glimpse of the soldiers' faces. A small gasps escapes her lips.

They're women, all of them.

t w e l v e

Felix, finally free from Kun's grasp, is panting, bracing his hands on his knees, his eyes searching Astra's. He opens his mouth, but he speaks so quietly, so that only she will hear. "That's the meander of parts," he mouths to her.

"What?" she mouths back.

"If you can tear your eyes away from the pretty snowflakes, Platoon," the woman's voice continues, "and get on with it, I'd appreciate it."

Astra turns her attention away from the woman, distracted for a second. She's right. The Colonist soldiers keep stopping as they drag Kun to the train's tracks, their progress halted by their curiosity. They lift their hands, palm up, trying to touch the snowflakes. They keep bringing their fingers close to their faces, no doubt wondering why there's nothing left once they catch the white dots that are drifting from the sky. They don't seem overly concerned about their prisoner -the most dangerous man in the One World is right now the most helpless one.

Kun's figure is drooping between them, and he has to be supported by the soldiers to stand upright, while his legs don't seem to be able to hold him up. But the Colonist army of women - *women! Astra still can't believe her eyes-* have their attention occupied elsewhere. By now, all of them are fascinated with the snow. And Kun's men... Kun's men are watching them, mouths agape, eyes darting from one woman to the other in awe and confusion. They're watching the ones who are leading their leader away easily, effortlessly. They're watching the ones who are playing with the snow. They're watching.

Astra smiles.

She steals a glance at Felix, and finds him staring intently at her, talking to her with just his eyes.

The men are waking up, they tell her. *Look at them. They've never imagined something like this could ever exist. That's how it worked for me as well.*

Yes, she answers him with a glance. *Let's hope it won't take them as long as it did you, toy soldier.*

Shut up, his eyes say.

They say other things as well, but she'd rather not think about those other things while they're fighting to stay alive. *If anyone needs to shut up, it's the tin soldier's eyes.*

She fights the urge to run over and punch him in the nose -although it looks like Kun has done a pretty nice job on it already. Even when they're talking like this, without words, why should she shut up when he says so? But there's the matter of the crazy woman to deal with first.

"Urania," Luke says to the crazy Colonist woman, bowing his head respectfully. Oh. *'That's the Commander of Mars.'* Urania, the Commander of Mars.

That's what Felix was trying to tell her. The Commander of Mars is a legend. She's some kind of a genius, apparently. Her name is mentioned all the time on the Terrestrial Channel -every day her enterprise seems to be inventing some new weapon or new chemical for the well-being of the people of the One World.

"Welcome back," Luke says.

"You could have fooled me," the woman replies, not unpleasantly, and then she turns her head and looks straight into Astra's eyes.

Astra takes a stumbling step back, her boots sinking in the snow up to her ankles.

What the...?

"I know you," she says to the woman. "You're one of the Rebels. I know you."

The Commander just stands there, staring at her. She doesn't assent. But she doesn't deny it either.

t h i r t e e n

tin soldier

"I know you," Astra says to the Commander of Mars. "You're one of the Rebels." Felix's heart gives a thud that reaches all the way up to his throat.

The Commander's back looks rigid from where Felix is standing. She's waiting for Astra to speak again.

And speak Astra does.

"Are you serious?" she says, sounding mad, but Felix can tell that for all her attitude, she's pretty badly shaken.

She's not the only one.

He had his father's throat locked between his elbow and his chest a moment ago. All the time, he'd been thinking back on Ulysses' words from the Vis, his words about the emptiness and the greed of Constantine's heart, about his own self being the most important thing in the world to him. About renouncing the father and the woman and the son whose mere existence could incriminate him, with no remorse.

The questions had been burning within him, he'd longed to confront his father, to ask him if he truly did all these things, but hadn't found a chance to. The man hadn't even admitted he was his father. While he was choking him, knowing he wouldn't kill him just yet, he'd finally found his opening. He had the Chairman at his mercy, after all. And no audience. Perfect.

"Is it true?" he'd gasped in Kun's ear as he was pushing the Chairman's face down in the snow, struggling to breathe almost as much as Kun, since the Chairman might have looked still on the outside, but his muscles were pushing to break free the whole time.

"I should have killed you when you were a baby," Kun had whispered through clenched teeth. "I shouldn't have let you live. You weren't supposed to exist. Even one small weakness is enough to conquer you, you know."

"Oh, I know," Felix said.

And that was all. He had his answer. He also had one first -and last- lesson from his own father. One lesson was enough. *One small weakness is enough to conquer you*. Felix, he was the weakness, apparently. And conquer he did.

Well, sort of. He wasn't exactly on top, but he wasn't dead either when the Commander of Mars arrived. Then her soldiers strapped Kun into the Arian Cuffs, especially designed in the Colonies. They got their name from the timer Greek word for mars, 'Ares' being Mars. They were designed there, on Mars. So that's what Kun was afraid of. Everyone in the military knows what the deal is with the Arian Cuffs: they don't come off as long as the 'confined' is alive. Removal equals death. And as long as they stay on, they control every part of the body and brain: submission and endless pain are at the command of a button. Felix doesn't know how he feels about that right now. The Arian Cuffs mean that Kun and his guards, as well as the Counsil members present, will be taken to Mars prison camps and from there judged under Mars laws. Maybe his entire Counsil, including the Venus-born spies, whoever they were. They plotted treason against their Planet as well, after all.

"It's not over," Kun had said just for Felix's ears as his ankles were being strapped into the Cuffs.

But Felix could argue that it is. Kun's reinforcements from the Colonies were blown to bits; Felix knows that was what he saw in the sky a few minutes ago. And he knows who it was that blew them up: the Commander of Mars, of course. It looked like a torrent of stars were falling from the sky, but he'd known at a glance these were no stars; it reminded him of the fleet of shuttles Steadfast had crashed all those years ago. That had looked exactly the same.

The Commander sure moved fast. And by look on her face right now, there isn't much she doesn't already know about this whole conspiracy.

After all, she did call him 'Con', short for Constantine, his real name before he changed it to 'Kun'. And she doesn't have the stunned look of someone who heard Ulysses' words for the first time. A sudden thought occurs to him. *Of course.* Felix will bet anything Urania has already seen Ulysses' Vis on the Clock somehow, and knows everything. Maybe she's in on the plan. Maybe she knows even more than what was on Ulysses' Vis. Maybe more than he, Felix, knows. It doesn't make sense, but she has that look about her. As though she's been hiding truths that have been itching to find their way out for a while.

The same look Astra had when he first met her.

Felix can't tear away his eyes from the form of his father being led away from the Perennial Site. He would have stayed like this, looking after his disappearing silhouette for hours, until the Mars soldiers led him to the Intergalactic Station, but suddenly Astra's voice penetrates his consciousness. He turns abruptly, to find her face to face with the Commander.

"You're one of the Rebels," Astra is saying calmly. The Commander just stares at her, shaking. That can't be right. Neither the shaking, nor the Rebel thing. *Can it?* "I know you."

It takes forever for Urania to reply. The one single person that the entire One World admires and fears, is staring at a mere slip of a girl, robbed of speech. Astra is looking at her with accusation in her eyes, waiting. Felix looks at her, and his heart lurches. He's never seen a more beautiful sight than Astra right now, braid encrusted with snowflakes, cotton pants soaked with ice, cheeks flushed, limbs trembling.

What does Urania see?

Finally she opens her lips, licks them once as though they've gone dry. "Yes, you do," she says. "You know me. You know."

"I know what?" Astra asks, when Urania doesn't say anything else.

"That I couldn't tell you," the Commander says to Astra. "I couldn't tell you of my relationship with Christopher. I had to hide the fact that you're my natural-born daughter. You'd be in too much danger until things... changed. And then they didn't change. Forgive me."

Astra swallows.

Felix -and everyone around him- is holding his breath.

"You're the ballerina," Astra says.

No one understands her, except Felix. Luke moves next to Astra, wrapping his arm around her shoulders. Maybe he thinks she's going crazy. Felix smiles. He's yet to see anyone going less crazy than Astra at this moment.

'My natural-born daughter' Urania said. So Urania is Steadfast's woman. Or was. *Oh stars.* She was a Rebel before she became Commander? The Commander of Mars and the Pirate were a

family. Urania and Steadfast. They were a couple. And they made Astra.

"So I remember you from the Rebel camps," Astra says again to the Commander.

Urania nods. "Yes, I was a Rebel," she says. "And the Commander of Mars. A Rebel on Earth and a Commander in the Colonies. I had to divide my time between the Colonies and the Planet; I was both."

And you couldn't be a mother too, whatever that word means, Felix thinks, but he doesn't speak.

"All these years..." Astra says. "You were there when I was a kid. I used to visit from the Settlements. I remember you now, you were always inside the cave. You knit me clothes. You taught me to draw, didn't you? When I was really small. Why the timers didn't you say anything all these years in the mountains? You could have..." Her phrase trails into silence.

The Commander doesn't answer. She doesn't defend herself. She just stands there, and starts making sniffling noises.

"Oh, for Jupiter's sake," Astra says. Then she leans in and hugs her.

fourteen

match girl

Astra hugs the Rebel woman who is now apparently the Commander of Mars -not to mention her mother- and is surprised to feel the woman's arms come around her back as she holds her there.

She faintly remembers a quiet, sad girl who sat alone for most of the day, but this woman is nothing like that: she is all warrior. Her hair is short, her braid gone, she's taller than Astra, and her arms are sinewy underneath her Colonist military suit. The woman with the flowing brown hair and the cotton pants she knew when she was a kid in the Rebel camp on the Alps bears very little resemblance to the Commander of Mars in front of her.

What seems like a million years later, the Commander is still holding Astra fast. When she finally lifts her face from Astra's shoulder, she doesn't remove her arms from around her, nor does she stop fingering the stray red hairs that have escaped Astra's braid.

"Sergeant Mache, Sergeant Enia?" She says it without looking away from Astra.

The two soldiers in the front snap to attention.

"You two will stay behind with me. The rest of you will accompany the ex-Chairman, and leave his guards here. I'll expect you back within the hour," the Commander says to her soldiers "Oh, wait."

Astra is beginning to remember.

The woman she remembers, the Rebel girl, as she was then -Ruth was her name- didn't speak. Now she realizes why. She's got the weird accent of the Far Colonies, and anyone would suspect her of being a Colonist the moment she opened her lips. Besides, she has the voice of a Commander. Was she a Commander back then? She did say she was both, but it's hard to believe such a thing was possible.

She hadn't really needed to speak back at the Rebel camp anyway, now that she thinks of it. When she was there, she used to hold Astra when she was crying and teach her how to braid her hair and sew up the holes in her father's tunic.

Not that Astra has had any experience with how a mother should act, but anyway... *Wait. Does that mean that I am half Mars-kind?*

The thought hits her hard and Astra gets dizzy, the ground taking a dive to the side, and stumbles. Felix's hand is there, warm and steady on her shoulder, his eyes looking into hers with concern.

"You ok?" he asks in a whisper.

She shrugs, noticing that he's beginning to shake from cold and blood loss and he's filthy with mud and dried blood. He's got a fat lip. His cheeks look white against the night sky, his gaze fierce, his eyes twin flames, their blue color fiercely brilliant in the darkness.

"Astra?" he insists.

"No," she tells him. Just 'no'. Just one word that shatters him.

Felix grimaces, taking a shuddering breath, but he doesn't get a chance to speak. Behind them, there's a dull bang, the muffled sound of a gun firing, then silence. They turn to see what's happened, and freeze.

One of Felix's cadets is lying in a pool of blood. Astra looks more closely and she sees that it's the boy who betrayed them, the one who turned his gun on Felix. His fellow cadets had struck him and he was unconscious all this time, but now... Now he's worse than unconscious.

Felix just stands there for a second, unable to move. Astra can't believe her eyes. *This can't be happening.*

"Malik!" Felix springs into motion, breaking into a run, stumbling and sliding on the ice because his legs, his whole body is shaking. He drops to his knees next to the dying cadet and places a hand behind his neck, lifting his head, but his skin is already turning grey. Even from here,

Astra can see that Malik's eyes are closed and his nostrils are still; he's not breathing.

"Somebody help me," Felix screams, burying his hands into Malik's suit, parting the torn Hydro jacket, and trying to stem the blood flowing from the gaping hole in the cadet's chest.

The Commander just watches them; it wasn't her doing, but she won't bestir herself to set things right. But next to her, one of her soldiers, the one she called Enia, is lowering her hand. A Colonist weapon is clasped in her fist.

"What did you *do*?" Felix shouts at her.

"He was close to death," Urania replies calmly, stepping closer to her Sergeant. "It was a mercy, considering what our laws foresee for traitors to the Peace of the One World," she adds with a glance at Kun. By now he's nothing but a faint silhouette among the flanks of her soldiers, fading into the night. It seems as if he disappears so easily, wiped off the face of the Planet. But what a toll of loss he's left behind him. "Everything that's happening here today is being broadcasted live to your Terrestrial Channel, you know that, yes? Everyone, including those of us on the Colonies that are tuned in to it, saw what he almost did. Saw what the ex-Chairman did. Everyone heard what Ulysses said about him. Those of us who didn't already know, that is."

Of course she knew, Astra realizes. It's not just the secret of her origin she's kept from her; it's the secrets of the world. She must have known Ulysses as well, maybe she'd been to the shack.

I shared the mountains with this woman. I shared her body. I shared my father. And she just gave the order to kill someone in cold blood. She's still talking about the Channel and Kun and the One Peace.

Of all the things she could tell me, that's all she wants to say right now. All she has to say.

"But now, finally, we have proof," Urania continues. "We have witnesses to his downfall, and that cannot be undone. It was my chance."

So that's what all this was to her? An unexpected bitterness pierces Astra's heart.

"Even now, our every word is made public," the Commander adds with a nod towards one of Kun's guards.

What does that mean? Is he carrying some sort of recording device on his suit? Felix nods, understanding, his eyes fixed on the soldier's face. It might be the goggles, Astra realizes. She wonders how the soldiers can even see properly through their tinted lenses, but she's pretty sure there are military data-rolls on there, and the soldiers receive coordinates and orders through them. Maybe they're also camcorders, feeding into the Terrestrial Channel? Most soldiers wear them. Maybe that's why Urania ordered Kun's guards to stay. So that their every word, every action will be broadcasted to the universe.

Astra's stomach turns, an acidic taste rising to her lips. Suddenly she wants to run over and rip every guard's goggles from their faces. Felix isn't wearing them, at least that's a relief.

"You didn't have to kill him; he wasn't the traitor himself, he was just acting on orders. He could have been saved, he could have-" Felix starts, his voice sounding gruff, close to breaking. His face looks ashen. His hands are still on the hole on Malik's chest, holding it closed, blood drying on his fingers.

"Lieutenant," the Commander interrupts him. "There's no time for that. Gather your war council, if you possibly can, and follow me. I'll wait for you to give the order."

"Go to Mercury," Felix tells her roundly.

Then he suddenly stills, as though what she said is taking a moment to sink in. He lifts his eyes to the Commander's face. "Wait, what?"

f i f t e e n

Felix is rooted to the ground, speechless. It's hard to wrap his mind around what's happened. Everything went down so quickly, he's hardly had time to catch his breath Every moment has brought a new change. Felix feels dizzy with blood loss and a sense of responsibility so huge it's almost overwhelming.

Thousands of guests and most of the Counsil are locked inside the Stadium, infected, a Rebel team along with them; Kun is a prisoner of Mars; the citizens of Earth must be freaking out everywhere by now, terrified by what they've watched on the Terrestrial Channel -but then again some of them, somewhere, might be waking up. This very minute.

Or maybe that's a bit of a stretch, and the Commander is right in her cynicism.

"Wake up, lieutenant. Do you think this Planet can wait for you to muse over your options?" Urania's low, commanding voice snaps him from his jumbled thoughts. He looks up to find her eyes fixed on his. They're Astra's eyes, the same hazel color, the same shape. "There will be riots breaking out in an hour, tops, all the way from Neo Tokyo to Europea. And there's no one to take charge, except for you. Don't you want this job?"

"I do *not* want the job," Felix says emphatically and Urania scoffs.

"Christopher should be here now," she says and Felix notices Astra flinch. Her lips are beginning to turn purple from the cold, since she is the only one not wearing a Hydro suit -except for Luke and the remaining Rebels.

"Yes, he should," Felix says dryly. He turns to his remaining cadets. "Soldiers, at ease."

That's not exactly an order. Well, it is, but it also is a trick.

A test.

After all, he, Felix, is the only loyal Lieutenant of the Planet's Military Forces present. He's the highest ranking official that doesn't stand accused of high treason. By rights, every soldier on this plain should obey him. *But let's see who actually does.*

He turns around to see who will obey the order. There are about forty soldiers left standing from the Chairman's personal Guard, and the eight cadets of his own squad. Kun's first general is dead and his sergeants are restrained by the Arian Cuffs.

About twenty-nine obey -thirty if he counts Astra, who doesn't know how to stand 'at ease', but he does count her, because if there is someone who should be part of his 'war council', as the Commander put it, it's her.

He waves a hand at them to approach. The Rebels stand aside, ready to help if they are needed, but not joining in.

"There we are," he says to Urania, with a flourishing gesture. "This is my war council, or whatever you want to call it. But with all due respect, Commander, it's not a war I'm after. Nor is it the killing of underage, ill-advised boys at a moment's notice, whatever their crimes. I'm definitely not a fan of how you handle things."

Cold sweat drenches him as he remembers what happened. He hasn't stopped shaking since the moment he knelt down to try to push Malik's skin back together. Yet the hole in the boy's chest was becoming bigger by the second, blood pouring from him, spilling on the ground. Wasted. It was as though the hole was gaping, opening to swallow Felix in its depths, taunting him. *It could have been you instead of him*, it seemed to say.

And then another thought shakes him.

It could have been him, Felix, instead of *her*. Instead of the Commander. He could have been the one to give the order to cancel a life.

Or it could have been him in Malik's boots, confused, led to betrayal because he believed the lies he'd been fed from infancy.

It could have been him in the place of one of the guards of the Chairman, shooting blindly at enemies he had no reason to hate, protecting the one who was planning to destroy them all.

Yes, it could just as well have been him in the Commander's shoes, ridding the Planet of the traitor, killing the killer, protecting the so-called peace by destroying it.

A few days ago there was absolutely no difference between himself and Malik. And the Commander of Mars, so smart, so talented, so much more enlightened than any of them... Killing a boy in cold blood. He's no better than her. A bit worse, in fact. Much more ignorant and powerless and stupid. So what if he's only killed in stimulations and they've done it in real life? What if it was Karim who pushed the rod into Steadfast's skin? It could easily have been Felix, he's done it a hundred times to others. He would have been doing it today to the Clockmaster, if things had gone as the old man had planned, if it hadn't been for Astra. If he was still in the Chairman's army. He's one with the guilty. He's them.

'Equal in guilt.'

So that's what the Rebel had meant.

A weight rolls off his shoulders, a weight heavier than the world. He hangs his head low, trying to hold onto that knowledge. Equal in guilt.

Equal in fault and betrayal and weakness. The Rebel had spoken of peace within, of changing inside first, then the world. And finally he's beginning to get it: he's carrying the darkness inside, the ugly blackness that was released when he learned the truth about his father; or the stupid indifference to human lives he'd been taught to show. All of this is living within him, and he's just now beginning to see it.

Soon enough, he'll get to battling it; to conquering it. To fighting it with all he's got.

'*One weakness is enough to conquer you,*' Kun had said to him. He meant the word as an insult to his son, but now Felix can hear a whole other meaning in it.

"Malik," he whispers, although Malik is beyond hearing. He, Felix, needs to hear it, though. "May we share forgiveness as we shared the guilt."

The Commander turns her head away, sighing. "You're dreaming of a bloodless revolution, just like Christopher," she says. She doesn't look much impressed, even though she's comparing him to Astra's father. It should be a compliment, but somehow it sounds like an insult. "Got him killed in the end," she adds dryly. "Much good *that* did to everyone. All we were left with was his loss. His vain loss."

"We'll see," Felix says, turning to the soldiers. The ones who haven't joined him aren't openly hostile as yet, but they don't move either. They are just watching through clouded, confused eyes, perhaps trying to decide, perhaps not. They're obviously afraid for their lives, but not sure if he's the one to follow. "Fall into ranks!" he shouts.

There is a bit of scuffling of boots and grunting, since the men belong to different regiments. The Rebels intervene, quite expertly, once they see that they're needed. Moving in perfect formation, they join the lines of the soldiers, nudging them into order. Finally the men untangle themselves enough to stand in a straight line. Felix sighs. *This is hopeless.*

It feels so strange, being the commanding officer to all these men, especially the Rebels. Now that they've joined ranks with the rest, he's even more intimidated. He's in awe of them -he even fears them, in a way. But now, he has to be their lieutenant. That's all there is to it.

"Turn off your goggles," he tells them and they do. "Now the others."

Some of the insubordinate guards do it by themselves, realizing the panic that broadcasting these moments could cause to the rest of the Planet and the One World, but three keep them on, squaring their shoulders in defiance.

Felix doesn't have time to react. Just a nod from the Commander, and her two soldiers are upon them, ripping their goggles off, strapping the Arian Cuffs on their ankles in no time.

"No!" Felix shouts.

There's a new authority in his voice that takes even him by surprise. '*Were you planning for him to take my place?*' Kun had asked Astra. Do you see anyone else here? her eyes had replied, shining, defiant.

He turns to the Commander, facing her straight in the eye. "I said their *goggles*. Just their goggles. You are not the Commander on this mountaintop on Earth. Understood?"

Urania gives no sign that she does. She's hardly looking at him, but her soldiers are.

"Release them," Felix commands them.

They don't, of course. They couldn't release them without killing them if they wanted to -not that they had any intention of following anybody's orders but their Commanders'-, so they stand still. What's been done can't be undone. *Merc.*

Felix passes a hand over his face. He feels his frustration scrape his throat raw, muscles coiling, cramping. Just as he's about to lose control, he runs his gaze around for inspiration. A calm, brown gaze catches his eye. Astra.

He focuses on her face, taking deep breaths, feeling his heart rate slow down to a heartbeat per second, not stopping, but never jumping erratically either.

Thank you, he mouths to her.

She just nods, and that's when he realizes how tired she must be, if she can't think of anything smart or annoying to say back. The Health Disc could do so much, after all, and her body can't have healed from the rod's electric shock so soon.

"Soldiers," he calls out in a loud, clear voice.

Everyone's eyes are glued to him. A tingle travels down his spine, watching all those faces watching him, waiting, blank. Karim's face has become one with the night, his hair dripping wet with snow, his round eyes glowing like coals. His lips are pursed, as if he's waiting to see when Felix will mess it all up.

Felix grits his teeth. He's got about one second before their attention starts to waver; less than that before he'll have to leap into action, if they have any hope of saving anyone inside or outside that Dome, including themselves. He takes a deep breath.

"The Chairman's time is over," he says, and most of the eyes that were fixed on his go dull, darting left and right. Astra clears her throat.

His eyes dart to her. She lifts her eyebrows.

What?

Her eyes drift towards Kun's soldiers. She tightens her lips.

Oh. He's supposed to think what *they* must be thinking right now. He knows what they're thinking. If there's one thing he knows, it's this.

He sets his teeth and starts talking. "You need to know some things about him," he starts again. "First and foremost, the Chairman can't, nor could he ever hear your thoughts. No one can. It's one of the lies we've been told. Lies." He remembers Ulysses' eyebrows meeting on the PR screen in the ice shack, as he bent down to whisper the word. His eyes find the Commander, who was watching him from the sidelines. She is listening intently.

"Think about it, think for yourselves. You can think whatever you like, your brain belongs just to you. Think about the world we live in. We can transport anywhere in the One World within minutes, but no one really communicates; we do things -well, the men do things, but we don't really feel anything. No one does. Animals are something we feed into our labs, losing entire species without a second thought; women and girls the same. Those that are thought to be criminals are kept in the Box, executed out of sight. But the laws against which we measure our justice, they are arbitrary at best-" He stops abruptly.

Someone exhales sharply. Everyone is still looking at him, their attention focused, but he turns and sees Astra's lips trembling, her eyes shining with tears. He hides a smile. It's what she said to him, word for word.

What, didn't she think he was paying attention? A soldier shuffles his feet.

Right. Keep talking.

"As you heard inside the Stadium, the Venus fleets might be heading our way even as we speak," he addresses his 'war council', as Urania called it. "They will be anticipating unrest all over the Planet after what's happened here today, and, with the Counsil in shreds, they will probably jump at the chance to take advantage of the uncertainty of our situation and attack as soon as possible, before we have any hope of assembling an army force, basic as it would be compared to their own. You may have realized by my previous orders that the Stadium is already infected with the nanovirus of the After Plague. It has therefore been sealed from inside to protect the rest of the population. The Chairman's plan has been put in motion."

He's never addressed soldiers in such a way before, so he hardly knows what he's saying. Everyone appears to be listening to him, though. Even the Commander. She has that calm, slightly mocking smile on her face, her lip curling on the left side, the rest of her mouth set grimly.

Let's see if we can make it slip an inch or two, he thinks. *Let's also see if there's any way in Mercury my plan will work.*

"In this I hope you will agree with me, even though I'm not your general or your superior in any way, that right now there is only one course of action. And to make that happen, I will need your absolute cooperation. The Planet will need it. Anyone who has any doubts as to following my orders, step back now."

He waits for a second. Then two.

No one steps back.

In fact, the opposite happens.

He turns to address them once more, when a movement across the plain catches his eye. Three of the five sergeants who have Arian Cuffs strapped around their ankles, the ones who had refused to take off their goggles at his command, start moving.

For a second they look as though they are having leg cramps or something. They would have looked pretty funny too, if the snow wasn't stained by blood all around them, as they're trying to shift their bodies with their feet confined like that. As it is, it's dead serious: they are trying to walk.

No, they are trying to walk *towards him*. First the one on the left takes a tiny step forward, then the other two do the same. The snow is thick by this point, pouring down in torrents from the skies, and their boots sink into it ankle-deep. Since the Cuffs are holding their ankles together, they can't lift their legs far enough out of the snow to walk.

The first soldier stumbles, tries to right himself, but then his other foot gets tangled in the snow and he falls with a thud, rolling a few paces down the slope. The other two follow him in a moment.

Everyone is watching, holding their breath.

The guards can't lift themselves up, although their hands are free, because as soon as they brace them on the ground to lift themselves up, they sink an inch more into the muddied snow.

"Kash, Karim," Felix says. Just their names. But his cadets realize what he wants them to do.

Without hesitating, the cadets run up the mountain to help Kun's guards to their feet.

Karim hesitates just for a split second, and turns to Felix. He gives him a look.

Stars, here we go, Felix thinks. *He'll say something stupid. Or worse, something smart.*

Then Karim winks.

He actually *winks* at him.

Crazy boy. Idiot.

He and Kash reach the guards and help them to their feet in a breath, and then they put their arms around their shoulders, supporting them as they walk towards Felix so that, hopefully, they might reach the new squad before the next year dawns. Still their progress is slow.

And then it happens. The impossible -or rather, one more impossible.

Three more soldiers from Kun's personal Guard, the ones who stood aside, refusing to obey Felix, break ranks and start walking towards Felix and his newly-formed platoon. The next minute, five more follow. They're privates, so they're not cuffed.

Felix keeps swallowing hard, not knowing what to say. He reaches out a hand to help one of the cuffed guards up the last steep slope.

"Thank you," the guard says, then snaps to attention. The Commander scoffs somewhere in the background. Felix ignores her.

"Everyone is needed, if we' re going to save our home." Blank looks met his eyes. "Earth," he adds as an explanation. "Earth is our home. Does anyone here think we can?" he yells.

The soldiers yell back that they do.

"I don't," Urania murmurs under her breath, but he hears her.

"Your daughter doesn't know when to shut up either," he whispers at her, his eyes wandering to Astra again. *Hold on a bit longer, match girl*, he told her silently. *We're almost done.* "I can see where she gets it from. Too bad *you* don't take after her in courage and compassion."

"What d'you want us to do?" Karim asks from his left.

"Seal the Pods," Felix replies. "Destroy them. Nothing can come out, nothing in. If Venus wants to invade Earth, let them take the long way. It should take them two months, if they are as great a force as they are rumored to be -more, probably. I'll transport to Headquarters, see if we can shut down the mainframe from there. Maybe we can keep the Terrestrial Pods open for inter-planetary transportation, but if we can't, we'll close them anyway. Luke," he turned to the Rebels, "we'll need some of your hackers, if you can spare them."

Luke nods, turning to his men.

The Commander is making a weird sound, half-choking, half-puffing in annoyance.

"Problem?" Felix turns to her.

"You're keeping me a prisoner here, Hunter?" she asks, trying to look as though she doesn't care either way, although she isn't fooling him for a second.

"Not if you leave right now," Felix replies.

Urania lifts her eyebrows slightly. "Will you wait for us to leave before you seal the Pods?" she asks imperiously.

Felix is beginning to get tired of her condescension. She is all but stranded on this Planet, yet she doesn't want to even look as if she's worried whether she gets back safely or not. Fine. He cares even less. "The train will reach the closest Pod, which I guess is at the Perennial Site, in about five minutes," he tells her carelessly. "You have four."

"Fair enough," the Commander replies, signaling to her remaining soldiers.

Felix drops the tone of his voice, taking a step towards her. "Commander, you know better than anyone how inadequate I am for this position."

"You won't always be," Urania says.

He shrugs. "Until that happens, I'm going to need help -a lot of help. I know now that you have an... interest in Earth," Urania's hand jerks where it's resting on her belt, and Felix lifts an eyebrow, but he doesn't comment on it. "So you're welcome to stay and help us. But if you'd rather go home, I won't keep you. We can communicate via Projections and Visuals, if you think you can trust me enough to allow me access to your mainframe."

"Spare me the melodramatics," Urania turns away from him, but Felix knows he's touched a nerve. "You realize that since Christopher, I'm as much Earth-kind as the rest of you are -even more. I've spent months on this Planet, I've ached for it, dreamed of it; I've wished for the stars to change and land me here forever. I've left half of my heart -and more- on it. For years."

She steals a glance at Astra, who is standing immobile, listening from a few steps away.

"But I can't desert my people. I have no means of returning if you shut off my access, now. So..." she turns and reaches out a hand to Astra.

Astra takes a step forward, then pauses, hesitating. Urania's face is transformed by a smile, but Astra's remains pale, tense, watching. She looks like she's struggling internally, her whole body coiled for fight.

And that's when his brain catches up to the meaning of the Commander's gesture and realization hits him like a punch in the stomach.

s i x t e e n

She wants to take my match girl with her. To Mars.

Felix turns on his heel, his back to the Commander and Astra. He kicks the snow with his boot, a muffled curse flying out of his lips.

"Nnn-" he stops himself just before screaming 'no!' at the top of his lungs, like a little kid.

Give her space, let her make up her own mind. After all, if there's one person in the whole One World who knows their own mind, it's her. If he wasn't being shattered into a million pieces, he'd laugh to see the Commander's face so vulnerable, open, for all the world to see, her eyes fixed on the slim figure walking towards her on the snow.

Astra is slowly making her way towards the Commander, stumbling a bit, but walking in a straight line, with her chin high, her braid swinging across her back. She takes her mother's hand in hers and stands close to her, their silhouettes merging into one against the backdrop of the night sky.

A sharp pain slices Felix's chest, and he takes a hissing breath, the icy air choking him as it enters his lungs.

His vision is growing blurry, his body going numb. His ribcage feels too tight, and his forehead is bathed in cold sweat. He opens his lips, but no air enters. *Is this how it feels to die?*

Then Astra opens her lips.

"No."

For the first time, Felix sees something like fear in the Commander's eyes. Relief washes over him, leaving him winded; relief so overwhelming his legs almost fold.

Ash. You'll be the death of me, match girl.

"I lost so many years with you," Urania is saying to her daughter in a whisper, lifting her hand to her hair. "It just wasn't possible, with Constantine there, and with Christopher's mission... It wasn't safe. But I won't lose any more. We never were what we were supposed to be, Christopher, you and I..."

"A family," Astra supplies and Felix has no idea what the word means, but he sees the Commander's eyes actually glaze over. When she speaks again, there is a catch in her voice.

"Yes," Urania says. "I have that chance now with you."

"I hardly know you," Astra replies, not unkindly.

"Forgive me." The Commander says, bending her head low. She has a soldier's body, toned, tall, and poised to fight, but now she looks like a beggar off the streets of the East Manhattan China Provinces. Her short silver hair clings to her brow as if she's sweating, and her face looks almost as young as Astra's. Her dark brown eyes have a fierce, glowing fire in their depths.

She takes a tentative step towards Astra, then hesitates. Felix can feel the tension in the air around him. Every single soldier is holding his or her breath. No one has ever seen the Commander hesitate. Ever. Or beg for anything, let alone forgiveness.

"This was the world we were born into," she says, her voice going soft, losing its harshness. For the first time, she sounds human. She sounds like Astra. "Full of secrets and deceit. This was how we were brought up to be."

"You don't have to be what you were taught," the match girl replies.

"I know that now," the Commander nods, choking back the emotion that quivers in her voice. "I know that, seeing what you have become, my beautiful, smart, brave daughter. You have become the most brilliant star, even though you grew up in the fiercest of nights. I want nothing more than to get to know you."

"I want that too," Astra says.

Urania waits. Felix can almost feel her impatience crackling in the chilly atmosphere. "But I have a family already."

And then her eyes wander over to Felix, and beside him Karim starts muttering 'enough already with the disgusting looks' under his breath, but Felix can't even tell him to shut his stupid face. He's frozen on the spot.

You mean me? he asks her with his eyes, although he can't see very well because of all the water in them.

You have no idea what a family is, do you? her eyes say back. *I don't either, but I want to find out.*

"Astra..." Urania starts talking again, and that's when Felix decides he's had enough.

"I hate to interrupt," he says, his boots crunching in the snow as he takes a few deliberate strides towards them, "but Astra's hurt and the Planet's not getting any safer while we're standing here, gawking at each other, so here's what's going to happen."

Urania glances his way; her face looks shattered, her expression blank, and Felix's heart goes out to her. *That's new. Feeling bad for someone else.* He doesn't care for the feeling, but he sort of likes that he can feel another's pain. It reminds him of something Astra would do.

"I'll take a small team with me to the Counsil Headquarters. The rest of the soldiers will divide the Military Stations among them, and make their way through each and every one, shutting down all the Pods there. As for the rest of you," he turns to the remaining guards who haven't joined his ranks, "you can go back to your Camps or stay here and freeze. No one will be arrested today, but if you don't comply, you will be court martialed. I don't expect you all to abandon everything you served under up to now, but I do expect you to do your best so that our people are saved. The self-serving treachery that brought us to this, the lowest point of human history, is the only thing that will absolutely not be tolerated."

He takes a deep breath. He has no idea how to go about doing this, mars help him.

"What about the infected?" It's a Rebel's voice. The question slices the silence and hangs in the air, frozen.

Felix stays silent for a few seconds, but his brain is working rapidly. The Dome includes Health Discs, which will last well above two weeks. The rest of the Planet is safe from the infection, for now. They have a little time, at least.

"As soon as there is a military plan in place," he says in a voice that makes him sound much surer of himself than he really is, "concerning the invasion, we will return and, with the help of the Commander..." He doesn't get to finish the sentence.

"You think I'll find a cure for the Virus, Hunter?" Urania interrupts him, her voice mocking. "Why in the stars would I help you right

Con's crimes? Especially after you've thrown me out of your Planet."

Felix purses his lips in a thin line. He feels the urge to grab the Commander by the lapels of her uniform and shake her until she sees reason, but he forces himself to stay calm.

"The Commander knows well," he starts, using the more formal third-person military address. He can see a mulish expression in Urania's eyes. *Damn it, what little precious time we have left is wasting.* "The Commander knows well that the Pods have to be sealed immediately, if we're to secure Earth's borders from the Venus Fleets. We may already be too late. She also knows that Earth's labs, without her help, have no hope of finding a cure for the nano Virus before everyone inside that Stadium is dead." He's almost shouting at the end.

That's all he can say. Just state simple facts, appeal to her humanity. Ironic as that sounds.

Urania starts to walk away.

"You're on your own, Hunter boy," she says. She sounds bitter -maybe over having lost Astra. Merc, he's got no time for this.

"Look, Commander-" he says, lowering his voice for her ears only.

The Commander shrugs her slim shoulders, and speaks without turning around to face him. "You're on your own," she repeats, at the same time that Karim starts roaring his name.

"Fel? *Fel!* Your merking girl has flipped."

"What-?" Felix's head whips around so fast he gets giddy. He follows Karim's gaze and swears under his breath. All he can see is Astra's silhouette getting smaller in the distance as she's running away from the soldiers, back towards the Stadium. *What is she-? Merc, no. She's heading for the Dome.* His whole body turns giddy with shock and pure horror, but his legs are already moving.

The next second he's sprinting towards the Stadium, after her, snow packing to the sides of his boots, his heart in his mouth.

"Astra!" Her name is ripped from his throat like a knife. Everything and everyone around him has disappeared. It's just him and the ice, and the endless distance separating him from Astra's running form in the distance.

She's almost reached the back door of the Stadium, but he's still running after her. He keeps slipping and falling on the ice, but he carries on with all he's got, his calves burning, his chest heaving. "Luke! *Luke!*" he screams.

He realizes that Luke's steps are stomping the snow right behind him, along with a pair of lighter ones, closer to him -Urania's. Karim joins him on the other side, his long legs swallowing the distance within seconds. The four of them run, their heavy breaths competing with the distance. Felix doesn't call out to Astra anymore, saving his breath for running. He pushes with all his strength, outrunning the other two, leaving them behind. He isn't the Academy's star lieutenant, the One World's most lethal weapon for nothing. The four speed towards the stadium, racing against the wind, Felix a few meters ahead of the others, but there is nothing anyone can do. They all know what's going to happen. No one can get to her in time.

She's already there.

She got a head start on them while they were talking, and nobody saw her head back to the Dome. And now she's in. Before anyone could reach her to stop her, she got inside the marking infected Dome.

"Ash," Felix gasps, out of breath, reaching the Dome.

He closes the distance to the back entrance of the Stadium in two strides, as the door slides shut. He whispers her name, and his breath clouds in front of him, like a living thing, tasting of desperation, but she's not there to hear him.

She's already disappeared amid a flurry of snowflakes twirling as the door slid shut on her back, shutting her in. She didn't once look back, although she must have heard him screaming her name. He reached the door just a few seconds after she went in. He flings himself to the manual handle, grasping it to wrench it open, then pushes with all his strength, until he gets lightheaded. His body slams into it again and again, and he hits the snow in a pile of what feels like broken bones, but he immediately picks himself back up, and hits the door again. *Open up, let me in!* He screams internally at it.

Karim roars his name somewhere behind him, but he doesn't stop. He bangs his shoulder against the steel, feeling his bones crack, his skin breaking. Strong hands grab his waist, his neck, restricting him, holding him back. He doesn't even care who it is that's stopping him from cracking his head open on the merking metal door.

"Luke, it's all on you, you bastard," he pants, struggling to free himself, to bang against the door some more, his voice a low rasp. He hardly knows what he's saying. "Your goons left the door open."

He winces as the arms restraining him clam like manacles around his biceps, whipping furiously around.

Urania is holding his left elbow in an iron grip and Luke, damn him, has an arm around his waist, cutting off his breathing, practically lifting him off his feet. They drag him back a few steps like that, legs kicking the air, arms flailing, and then shove him to the ground.

His butt hits the snow hard, and for a moment he just sits there, stunned, drawing his legs to his chest, trying to take a breath.

"Felix, I'm so sorry. The Dome couldn't be sealed from both sides," Luke starts saying, his breath coming in short gasps. His voice sounds broken, lifeless. "That would condemn them to certain death in there. They just shut it from inside -Astra must have realized."

Felix gets up and lets a string of curses fly, punching the snow. His voice is shaky. His clothes are too tight, he can't breathe. The cold air is stifling him, drowning him. He feels a bitter laugh that borders on hysteria bubble up in his chest. So that's it. That's how he loses her. Not by the Chairman's bullet or the guards' tasers. Not by drowning in ice, or by kissing. By her own free will.

She walked in, the match girl.

Just simply walked into the Dome full of infected people, without a backward glance.

All this time, while he and Urania had been talking like idiots, pointless, meaningless words, she was slowly making her way across the snow towards the Stadium. By the time Karim realized what was happening, she was just a few steps away from the door.

She didn't even look behind, no matter how loudly I was screaming her name. No matter how hard my boots slapped the snow, running, trying to reach her, I was too late. She just opened it and walked in.

He can't understand how a thing like that could happen, how she slipped right through their fingers. She just walked inside the sealed Dome, in plain sight. He lost her within seconds. *What was she thinking?*

Of course, he knows exactly what she was thinking. He knows why she did it. He knows it as well as if she'd told him, but his head is bursting, he can't wrap his mind around it.

She wanted to give Urania a reason to find the cure. It's as simple as that.

She went in to do what *he* should have done, what he should have been doing all this time rather than just stand there, discussing strategies with the Commander. While he was talking, she sprang to action to save the people -*his* people. To comfort them, to talk to them like a human being, to give them hope. As always, she had the presence of mind and the compassion to do what no one else had the guts to do. Neither him, nor Urania.

By the looks of her, the Commander is devastated. Will she still withhold the means to find the cure? If it's possible one exists, that is. But at least, Urania will not pretend indifference any longer. Astra has made sure of that. She might even get straight to work, although who knows how many months it will take for her scientists to come up with an antidote.

Felix's gut clenches at the thought. Because there's one thing that Astra may have not known as she sped for the Dome:

Some of the infected in there won't survive the time the cure will take to arrive from Mars. Most of them, reinforced by years of taking the Health Discs, will probably last long enough. But she, Astra, will be among those who won't survive.

She hasn't taken Health Discs regularly in ages, besides she's been seriously injured and out in the cold with no protection whatsoever. She won't last a day once she's infected; she'll die within hours. The Plague is meant to take down all those Elite who haven't been sick or hurt one day in their lives. And she's nowhere near as strong, especially now.

Something tells him that even if she suspected that was the case, it would have made no difference.

Stupid, mad, necessary sacrifice.

The shame is killing him -among other things.

Felix slides back down to the ground, facing away from door, from his blurry reflection on its sleek surface, struggling to breathe past the dry sobs that wrack his body.

Astra knew that not one of them would have gone inside, even if she had suggested it. Or they would have stood there and talked for ages, while the Elite guests and their children were trapped in there. So, Astra-like, she just walked in.

No announcements, no goodbyes.

Dammit, match girl.

tin soldier

"I'll get it."

"What?" Felix's head snaps up.

"I'll have what you need in two weeks, Lieutenant," the Commander says in a flat, dead voice. She looks numb, her face wearing a shuttered expression. She's still on her knees, hasn't bothered to pick herself up from when she was trying to restrain him.

He looks at her, eyes widening for a moment. Does she mean... *It can't be*. Is she talking about the cure? "In two wee-?" In two weeks. He rises to his feet gingerly.

Still too late for the match girl. But incredibly soon for the Planet.

"Thank you," he says, inclining his head slightly.

She shrugs, motioning to her two sergeants to follow her. She picks herself from the ground unceremoniously, and starts walking towards the train tracks, without waiting for him. But after a few paces, she turns back to face Felix.

"Hunter," she says. Felix's eyes fly to her face. "This right here is the first true alliance of the One World," she says. "Everything up to now has been pretend, in case you didn't know. Now it begins. And it begins with us."

Because of Astra.

"What does?" Felix asks.

"The One Peace, of course," she replies. "The real peace."

"And goodwill to men," Felix mumbles, remembering a phrase he read in a book, in the Library of Truth. The bitterness in his own voice surprises him.

Not without her! He wants to scream at the top of his lungs. Not merking without her.

Everything happens in slow motion from then on. Felix is in a daze, hardly aware of the soldiers yelling questions at him, hardly feeling his legs move as he starts to take command of his Platoon. Just as Urania's form disappears across the mountain plains, Felix gathers his new recruits and follows.

"Come stay with me at Ulysses' shack," Felix says to Luke before he leaves the mountaintop. "After I do everything I have to do, I think I'll go back there and... wait."

Luke's eyes are dry, but his face has taken on a pale, grayish color, his lips set in a thin line. He shakes his head. Most of the Rebels are already in their ranks, ready to follow Felix, but Luke hasn't moved.

"Pretty soon it won't be a matter of minutes to come and go wherever we please," Felix continues. "I... I'll need you."

"I'll be here," Luke replies calmly, and Felix suddenly realizes that he doesn't mean it just figuratively, but that he is actually going to set camp right there, in the arctic plains, and wait outside the stadium for the cure. He means he'll stay here. Guarding Astra.

Felix just nods and doesn't press him any further.

Luke opens his lips, but he changes his mind and doesn't say anything. He grips Felix's shoulder and squeezes tight. Then he lets go without another word.

The Commander of Mars and her sergeants board the train to the Intergalactic Station, which contains a Pod that will take her to her Colony - that's how they arrived too. They ride the train together, Felix, the Commander and the new platoon up to a point, the soldiers seating themselves a booth away, to give them privacy.

Not that it's privacy Urania is after.

She nearly breaks his eardrums, yelling through her comm. at her engineers to get cracking on those lab tests, even as she's leaping onto the moving train. Both she and Felix know it won't be fast enough, no matter what the Commander does.

Felix tells her he'll give her ten more minutes before he shuts down the Pod, feeling sorry for her. She tells him to go do something to himself that he doesn't quite understand, or how it would work if he should attempt it, and turns her head away. He can see her reflection on the glass. Her cheeks are wet with tears.

Shortly after the Commander and her sergeants disembark, Felix and his newly-formed Platoon get off at the closest Pod. They immediately transfer to the Headquarters.

There are no speeches this time. No battles to be fought either. Only an eerie silence and a heavy feeling hanging in the atmosphere, the promise of change, or the promise of doom.

It seems that the Chairman's absence is haunting the entire Planet, making everything lighter and heavier at the same time. There's an uncertainty that hangs in the air, and it becomes almost suffocating with every passing moment. As though the very existence of every single person on the Planet hangs in the balance.

Which it does.

There's a clock, more immense and more sinister than the one Felix made for the Perennial, tick-tocking its way to the deadline for all of their lives. Felix tries to keep his thoughts clear, to not think of the match girl and the Venus threat. To only thing about the next step.

Quick as lightning, he gives the order, and Karim and two Rebels barge into the 612th floor of the Headquarters Building and hold what's left of the Chairman's Counsil and the rest of the workers at gunpoint -the rest escaped as soon as they saw what was happening at the Perennial Site. Felix and the hackers work briskly on shutting down the Main Pods of the Planet's Cabinet Offices and Central Military Spots. It takes them less than two hours.

Right about then, the signals from the Visuals from the rest of his soldiers reporting back start blinking on Felix's Portable PR -he hasn't worn his goggles in ages, but he did take his Portable with him. He opens them, running through them all with satisfaction. It's done. His orders have been carried out: every Military Base is sealed. They had to restrict inter-Earth transportation on a major scale, although they didn't disable it entirely, which might end up being a life-saver. In any case, it's a small price to pay for safety.

e i g h t e e n

Seven hours later, Felix transports back to the ice shack. He left the shack's Pod open. He has that stupid, irrational hope that she'll come back to the shack somehow; he can't bring himself to believe he'll never see her again. He can't bring himself to shut off the only way she could come back to him, although he knows it will never happen.

He is just stepping out of the Pod inside the shack, when the PR on the wall blinks. Felix cues it, and sees Kash's serious face looking up at him from the West Indian Main Military Base. Felix waits for him to report, but Kash looks exhausted, at breaking point.

"What are my orders?" is all Kash asks, forgetting to address him formally. He looks so different, it's hard to imagine he was one of Kun's Drones just a few days ago. If his heart wasn't torn in a million pieces, Felix would be proud.

"Just rest for now," Felix says simply, before remembering Kash has no idea what that means. "Tomorrow we'll regroup, see what kind of mess we've gotten ourselves in. I'll broadcast the news on the Channel. We need to start pulling Kun's minions off the Counsil, and electing new ones. I'll get in touch with Luke, he'll know where to start. Then, I have to announce the alliance with the Commander of Mars, and send out an official memo about the cure as soon as I have news from the Commander. Everyone must know about the After Plague by now."

He sighs, grabbing at his hair. Kash is waiting, a rather blank expression on his face. Felix can see Karim hovering in the distance, walking in and out of frame, listening to their conversation, but looking away. *He doesn't want to talk to me yet; he needs time to accept what's happened, to accept that the previous regime is over and that we are in charge now. He'll have to hurry. Whatever procedure his thick brain needs to get through to accept that things are changing -and we're the ones changing them- has to happen sooner rather than later.* But he's letting him be for now.

"Sorry," Felix says to Kash. "I'm thinking out loud. I've no idea what I'm... I'll think it over and brief you tomorrow. Just follow Kun's guards to their own barracks and stay there. You won't be safe anywhere else. Repeat the order to the idiot pacing right behind you, make sure he and the rest follow. Stay put until I have the Counsil under control, then we'll start."

"Yes, sir, Lieutenant Hunter, sir," Kash says somberly, saluting. "Logging off."

"Shut up," Felix replies.

nineteen

If he was being honest with himself, which he is trying to be, Felix would admit that from the first moment he boarded the Terrestrial train to get to the Perennial site, almost a day ago, his mind has been on the Clockmaster's ice shack. He's been missing it so much it's almost hurting him physically.

Even while he was inside the Dome, waiting below-stage, every time he so much as blinked, the arches of the Library of Truth would appear before his eyes uninvited; he'd see in front of him Astra's stupid heater, the silly green door, those tiny blinking lights.

He'd catch himself thinking of it. Even in the middle of fighting, bullets grazing his ears and blood obscuring his vision, his brain would go: 'I wish I was home right now'.

Which is ridiculous.

He hasn't had a home, ever. The closest he had to it was the Academy, but no one could accuse him of feeling at home in there. The whole concept is foreign. It's for ignorant kids and weak women.

Not that they have a home either, what with occupying those suffocating small rooms, packed in huts in the Islands for ten years at a time, or living in the squalor of the Settlements, which any woman would be lucky to survive for more than five.

Yet here he is, less than twenty-four hours later, seated at Ulysses' timer table, sulking at his own reflection on the window. There's absolute silence in here. No PR droning on in the next room, no fire sizzling in the heater, no Astra to raise all kinds of hell riding her wheeled-board game. The wind outside is howling.

He can almost hear the rhythmic thump-thumping of his heart.

His reflection on the dark glass gets ugly, then blurry. Merc. He's crying again. He shouldn't be crying; he's just come back from saving the Planet, for mars' sake. Maybe the entire One World. He's certainly bought another few months for Earth, to say the least.

He should have known, he thinks half an hour later, when he finally manages to lift his forehead from his folded arms. Christopher's entire existence was about sacrifice, as was Ulysses'. All the signs had been pointing to this: in order to make a big change in the world, he'd have to lose something big.

He was prepared to lose everything, his own life even; everything except that. Except her.

Get a grip.

He can't even hear her voice in his head anymore. He hunches over, tears dripping on the table, shoulders shaking, and lets the grief wash over him. She was never supposed to be the sacrifice.

Anything else, just not her.

He has lived the greatest part of his life with a silent heart in his chest, a numb brain in his head, an empty stomach in his belly. Now he's going to have to learn to live without breathing.

Live without air.

He should rest, too.

He should lay his body on the floor, take off his wet, muddy suit, turn the heater on, tend to the wound on his arm. Run down to the Library to try to find any clues as to what he's supposed to do.

Try to live-Vis with someone on the Counsil. There have to be some people on his side in there; not everyone had to be held at gunpoint when he walked in Headquarters. A few even nodded to him, quietly, slightly, as though they were afraid to be seen by their fellow Counsil members, showing him their allegiance any way they could. Maybe Ulysses' voice broadcast from the Perennial Site had made them start thinking. Or maybe they were scared for their lives. Of course the most influential members are in the Stadium, slowly dying.

Oh, stars. Astra, too.

Slowly dying.

And he's just sitting here, helpless, useless.

So many things have to be done, but all he can do is mourn the one life that matters the most. Get up, idiot, Astra's voice, faint, says into his brain. What kind of loser sits on the floor crying when there's a war waiting to be fought? And over a girl too?

Hold on.

There might be a way to talk to Astra and the population inside the Stadium. He could do it via the Clock's PR -it will be easy to reverse it so that he can send a message. They can't have shut it down inside the Dome, why would they?

He jumps to his feet.

His muscles scream in protest. His arm's wound, unattended, is stinging like mercury as the dried blood pulls at his skin with every movement. His stomach has long since been resigned to feeling achingly hollow. But none of this matters now that this idea has occurred to him. Every single pain in his body fades, and he feels fine.

For the first time in hours he feels it's all right to take a shuddering breath. *Stay alive, match girl, I'm coming*, he thinks at her. *Just stay alive.*

He lifts his eyes to the window in passing, flinching slightly at the reflection of a tall, mud-covered stranger that pierces him with haunted eyes. It's him. He doesn't recognize his own reflection.

He sighs and starts taking off his tight-fitting Hydro jacket so that he can get to work, looking absently towards the pitch black sky, another annoying habit Astra passed on to him, when something catches his eye. His hand freezes mid-air.

In the flash of a second, there's a small thump against the glass to his left. His eyes dart to the other window. Felix exhales sharply. He freezes.

The breath dies in his throat for the second time in a single day.

twenty

tin soldier

A fistful of snow bursts against the windowpane of the shack's front room, showering the glass in shards of ice. Felix, shaken out of his daze, peels himself from his seat. He runs out into the hall and grabs the handle of the stupid, green wooden door.

He fumbles with it, cursing under his breath, because this is no time to be figuring out timer stuff.

Finally he gets it open and flings it aside with a loud bang, stepping out. A blast of icy air hits him and his legs sink into the snow almost up to the knees, but he hardly notices. He starts trudging forward, the fierce wind slicing at his face, snowflakes hitting him like tiny knives, his cheeks stinging with cold.

He stumbles, sinking up to his hips in the snow, falling to his knees, then gets back up. Cold seep through his cotton pants, but he's got bigger problems right now. He's trying to cry out, but there's no voice left in his throat. It's scraped raw.

"Ash," he ends up murmuring through chattering teeth.

He's sure he's dreaming. Or gone mad, delusional with grief. Not that he minds.

He thought he saw her red hair through the window. For a moment, a crazy moment, he thought it was she who threw the snowball at his window. Who else in the world would do a thing like that? But it's crazy. Insane. It can't be true. His match girl is locked inside the Stadium, miles from here, dying. He's lost so much blood he's hallucinating.

Still, he pushes on through the ice, the snow falling so heavily that he can hardly see in front of him. When he collides with something solid, he draws his body up and wraps his arms around it, holding fast.

A few hours ago he thought that finally his heart was beating normally; he thought his heartbeat had become even. Well, he was wrong.

It's going crazy now, a million beats per second, threatening to rip right out of his chest. Because the solid mass he's holding... It feels like he's holding *her*. Astra. It's the most realistic hallucination.

He passes his hands all over her body, looking for the well-known shape of her shoulders, her waist, her wrists. He dusts the snow out of his eyes, trying to find her red hair beneath the blanket of white that's covering them both.

Then.

"Felix," Astra's voice says quietly.

The next second his lips have found hers and he's tasting the cold on her cheeks, the snowflakes that have landed on her eyelashes. They sink to their knees together, and he grabs her chin with two fingers, catching her against him, tipping her head back as he bends down to fit his head to hers. This time the kiss is different.

He sighs against her lips, burying his long fingers in her wet hair, wrapping himself around her. Her feel, her smell, her touch. He's falling apart right there, in her arms, and he doesn't want to stop.

It's not like the first time. No one is watching except the wilderness. And it's not a felony; it's a dream. He feels her respond to his hunger, he tastes his own tears on her lips. He presses her to him, afraid to stop touching her in case she disappears, but her hands come around his waist as well. They feel thin as branches, coated with icicles, but right now they are the only thing holding him together. He bends his head to hers, gasping for breath, and lets all the pain disappear into their melding bodies.

How is this real? *It's not, it's a dream. It's the best dream anyone ever had.* They part, gasping, foreheads leaning against each other. Then, his lips still tingling from kissing her, he takes a deep, shuddering breath. And starts yelling at her.

His only excuse, if there is any, is that he's still sure she's a hallucination -and it's a pretty lame excuse at that. But it's only the fact that he can see here in front of him that makes all his desperation bubble to the surface. He never knew he could feel like this, anger and pain and despair pouring out of him like a volcano. It feels good. Well, not good exactly. It feels alive.

"Do you think I'm some kind of Drone, match girl?" he explodes, letting go of her hands, spitting snowflakes with every word. "This is the second time you've abandoned me. You just think I'll sit around here forever, waiting for you. You've never given a thought to what you do to me every time you merking disappear, you've never even *cared...*"

He has to stop to take a breath. He can't breathe, he's drowning. Tears freeze his eyes shut and he has to blink several painful times before he can see well enough to discern the dark lump in the shape of her body, crumpled on the snow in front of him.

"You'd prefer if I was lying dead on the ice back there on the mountain, wouldn't you? I mean nothing to you," he yells, feeling the veins pop out on his neck. "*Nothing.*"

He's even more convinced that she's a phantom, because she doesn't say anything, not a word. She just stands there, silent, un-Astra like, and lets his words wash over her. And when he grabs her arms and starts shaking her, she doesn't resist. She feels like a shell in his fingers, boneless, insubstantial.

"You didn't even *think* what it would do to me, to watch you walk into the Dome. To run after you, knowing I'd be too late... To watch you die all over again. You didn't..." he's crying so hard he can't speak. "Astra, you didn't even look back once. You'd have looked back for one of your... Rebels."

Something warm drops on his hand, and he sees a wetness glistening on it. A tear. He swipes at his cheek furiously.

"It's all you. You made my heart beat," he tells her, lowering his voice. His throat is burning. He reaches for her hand and brings it to his chest. He holds it there, his skin burning hot against her icy cold fingers. "I wish you'd never messed with me in the first place. Feel it now, it's bleeding. You did that too, match girl."

He can't even feel the weight of her fingers on his chest -and how could he? She's just a figment of his imagination. He can't get up, he can't stop shaking. He's just numb.

"Aren't you scared to touch me?" Astra's voice says, sounding soft and scared.

Felix sits up, parting her curls frantically, wiping the snow off her clammy forehead.

This is no dream, he thinks in a daze. *This is her. This is... What? A miracle?*

"Aren't you...?" Astra begins again.

He cuts her off. "Do I look scared?" The words come out choked, gruff.

"I can't see your face," Astra says, "there's snow in my eyes."

He grabs her from the waist and stands up, heading for the shack. He feels the weight of her body on his arm, and hoists her up, gritting his teeth in the effort it takes to walk through the blizzard. Her legs are hardly working, so he tries to lift her off her feet, clutching her to him, her head on his shoulder. *If this is the product of madness, let me never be sane again.*

"How did you get here?" he asks her, trying to dispel the feeling that he's crossed to another dimension where the impossible can happen.

"I couldn't get into any of the Pods in the Stadium," Astra says, her voice sounding stiff, as if her lips are covered in crystals *-I couldn't imagine that, could I?* Felix thinks, intelligently. "So I got out of one of the back doors that were left open and took the train, then walked the slope up to the shack. I th-threw snowballs at your window, you t-tin s-s..." Her teeth are chattering.

"You... walked up to...?"

He pushes his hip hard into the green door to open it, and places a hand on her back so that the wind won't snatch her from his arms before he can get her inside.

Maybe it *is* a dream after all; she feels so slight in his arms, as though she could slip through his fingers any second. She walked in the night, during a blizzard, to get to him? Is that even possible?

Well, she always was crazy, his match girl, there's no denying that. Even so...

He doesn't get to finish his train of thought. Without a sound, Astra collapses against him, her body sort of folding on in itself and he has barely time to catch her before she tumbles headlong onto the floor of the shack. A few stray snowflakes have followed them in, and the floorboards at the entrance are soaked, slippery with melting water.

Felix carries her into the table-room in two long strides and lays her on a chair. Then he runs to get the heater, which he places right next to her seat, almost touching her legs. Her braid is dark with snow, her face soaked, her pants and tunic clinging to her skin.

He starts rubbing her arms with his hands, not bothering to wipe the fresh tears that are coursing down his cheeks. His fingers tighten for a moment on her elbow, and he runs his thumb back and forth across her arm. He shuts his eyes, holding on to her for dear life. Her skin is still as cold as ice. Frantic, he hugs her to him, trying to warm her up, holding on to her so tightly against his chest, he's probably crushing her bones.

She murmurs something and he lets go, reluctantly. As soon as she can sit up by herself, he takes a step back, giving her space. She clears her throat, pushing a few wet strands of hair away from her eyes.

"Are you... are you any better?" he asks tightly.

"Not really," she replies, tucking her hands between her knees. "Just let me breathe, ok?" She takes off her boots and rests her stockinged feet right on the heater. *She'll burn her toes*, he thinks, but then she lets out a relieved sigh, closing her eyes and taking a shuddering breath. He has to look away; just watching her pierces him through.

"Sorry," he says.

"Did I say I minded?"

"Let me help. What can I do?" A muscle ticks in his jaw.

"You can come here," she replies. "Why did you leave in the first place?"

"I'm not the one who left," he mumbles, but he kneels beside her and runs his long fingers up and down her arms, warming her frozen skin. He feels her tremble beneath the wet Rebel tunic that's clinging to her body. "I swear you'll drive me crazy, match girl."

"I'm not sick, you know," she says suddenly. She's leaning her head on her bent elbows, as though she's too exhausted to hold it up, but she lifts her face to his. Her eyes are dark, unfathomable pools. "I didn't get infected. I'm not stupid."

"What did I say about calling yourself that?" Now he's really mad. Well, at least that's better than being sad. Maybe the imaginary match girl will keep him mad, like she always does, so he won't slip into that bottomless despair again.

"I just snatched a pair of goggles your soldiers had thrown away on the snow before I ran into the Stadium," Astra says. What she says sounds far too logical to be a delusion. "Did you see that as you were chasing me like a madman? And in front of your new recruits! They must have been seriously impressed, tin soldier."

She sounds sarcastic and full of cheek. She sounds... like Astra. Felix sits up on haunches, looking into her eyes. *Wait, what did she say?*

"You mean... you really aren't sick?" he repeats.

"The goggles seal tightly around your skin, no matter the size of the head you put them on, right? So I put them over my mouth and nose. It made it a bit hard to talk to Matt and the others, but I managed it. Nothing came in," she adds. "I'd thought of everything before I acted." She stops talking for a minute; there's absolute silence. "I told you *I'm* not stupid. I didn't say you weren't." She adds in a minute, but her voice sounds soft, almost tender.

"We all know I am," he murmurs.

"I had to go in there, you know I did," she says quickly. "Someone had to, or Urania wouldn't help us. And you... you're too important to risk your life."

A strangled sound like a whimper escapes him, but she doesn't let him speak. *'You're too important...'* His mind flashes to the Rebel's dead body on the snow. That's someone he'd call important. Not him, Felix.

"So I went. I wasn't planning on coming back so quickly, but there is something I had to tell you. Listen, ok?" As if he wasn't all ears already, focused on her every word. "Do you know what the people in there said to me as soon as I told them what had happened? They said, go back out and tell him: we'll be your weapons."

He's left speechless for a moment. He clears his throat; it's hard to talk. "You thought of all of that by yourself?" He's never felt more admiration for anyone. Nor has he felt more stupid or inadequate or humbled. "Wait. Did... did they actually say that?"

"Some of them did. None of the Elite, of course, they were all just looking around with wide eyes. But the rest of them... You told them the truth. Nothing is more powerful than that. They saw it. They recognized your honesty. I mean, nobody would act that stupid unless they were being honest." Felix winces, but a smile is beginning to form on his cracked lips. "Besides, Felix..."

"Besides?" Felix prompts, his voice shaky from hearing his name on her lips again.

"Almost everyone knows someone who was sent to the prison camps or the Box for no reason. Or someone who was made into a murderer, or someone who became a Felon overnight, because he said the wrong thing about the Chairman."

Felix shuts his eyes. The kid who yelled 'Drone' at one of the soldiers and was dead a moment later still haunts him. He saw that. He was there. A sick feeling begins at the pit of his stomach, and he leans his head down, fighting a sudden nausea. Also, hiding his face from her.

"Anyway," Astra goes on, "I said there's no need for that. Felix is no Constantine. We'll live; the tin soldier gave his word. He'll keep it."

"*Your* tin soldier," he says. She doesn't say anything in reply. "I'm sorry about yelling at you," he starts again. "About the things I said. I was just..."

"You know you mean everything to me," she interrupts him. "You're so stupid to even doubt that..."

Felix doesn't even hear the end of her sentence. He's on his feet, reaching a hand behind her neck to bring her face up to his, and then he's kissing her on the mouth fiercely, hungrily, his tears mixing with her taste.

"I am sorry," he whispers into her mouth. "I'm so sorry." His voice sounds wet with tears, his nose clogged. He doesn't even care. "I'm sorry."

He wants to apologize for Jonas and Steadfast and Malik and Urania, but there are no words. He can't even begin to imagine the pain she must be in. "Please don't hurt anymore."

His chest shudders with silent sobs and she lays her hand lightly on his arm, between them, her warmth seeping through his shirt until the crying start subsiding. He sniffles. Her fingers are cold as icicles, but his skin feels scorched wherever her hands touch him, as though she's made entirely of fire. They both are. They melt into each other, and he pulls her to him until Astra topples from her chair, and Felix cradles her on his chest as they fall backwards onto the wooden floor. The same floor they nearly died on the first day he met her. A laugh escapes their joined lips.

"Remember when I said I hated you?" she murmurs into his neck. Her braid is draped across him as it's drying out, auburn tendrils coiling around his upper arm.

"Vividly," he replies, smiling. Of course he remembers. He could think of little else when he thought he'd lost her.

"What's the opposite of hate?" she asks and he sighs in happiness, because for once he knows the answer.

"Love," he says, tasting the unfamiliar word as it rolls off his tongue. He likes its sound. "Love," he repeats again for good measure.

He feels that a dam has broken inside his chest and all that's good and new will flow out of it.

"No, that's not it," Astra says infuriatingly, and her eyebrows meet in concentration.

Felix laughs aloud. He loves her, that's what it is. *I love her.*

Goose bumps break out all over his skin. Then Astra speaks again, and instead of getting mad at her, he melts.

"Wait, I got it," Astra says. "I belong with you."

twenty-one

Tomorrow will officially be the first day of the year twenty-five twenty-five. The year that will be different. It might also be his last day alive, but he won't think about it now.

Felix will start working tomorrow, working as he's never worked before.

There is so much he has to do. There are the women's Settlements to demolish, the Health Discs to destroy, there is a cure to find. The Counsil seats need to be redistributed, and a legitimate voting system for the Planet's Elite established. Or should the class of the Elite be done with altogether? He'll have to look into Ulysses' Greek books for inspiration.

There's a war to fight.

So many things to change, so many battles to win. How will he even know where to start?

Steadfast's memory must be restored; maybe he'll start from there. And not only that, but the people of the One World will trust Steadfast's daughter as soon as the truth comes out about what she and her father did. Their sacrifices. Just by having her by his side, his position will be that much stronger, just because of her. There must be some who suspected the truth even before now, some who tried to think beyond the lies they were fed.

Earth couldn't have been turned into a Planet of imbeciles within a few decades, could it?

Then again, he was a Drone before Astra found him.

Which reminds him, he has the Army to reform as well. These boys need to be educated, trained, prepared. Woken.

He has treasures to discover in Ulysses' Library. He has to change the laws -if any actually exist, because he has a suspicion that the Counsil just does whatever the merc it wants and calls it legal.

He has the crimes of the previous Counsil to deal with, the death of a cadet to mourn, Karim's huge eyes full of questions to answer to.

He has Ursa to protect, to make sure she's alive somewhere out in the mountains, after saving their hides. He has to make sure she's not the last Polar bear. He has to make sure she's the first. The first of the new world he'll help build, with many white furry babies to play snowball fights with, and fish to eat and other animals to keep their world alive.

He has no idea how to go about doing any of that, of course. He'll have to ask the Commander for advice and to bury himself into the Library of

Truth for months and months, if he wants to call himself a true Soldier. He doesn't dare call himself anything else. At least he can't call himself a Drone -not anymore. The match girl saw to that.

Tomorrow he'll send a Vis to the former guards of the Chairman, set up their first official hearing. Tomorrow he'll start turning the world upside down.

But for now he's just feeling Astra's warm body against his, safe, alive, familiar. For now he's just burying himself in her words, tightening his arms around her, closing his eyes in happiness. Letting out a breath of pure joy.

For now he's just hers. As he will always be.

twenty-two

match girl

I belong with you.

These words came out of her lips only a moment ago. She can't feel her fingers, her body is still tingling from the electric shock and her heart feels shredded, bruised from everything she's been through today.

Jonas dying in her arms.

Urania's cold, stricken features.

Felix creating an army.

Kun -rendered irrelevant within a few seconds.

Ulysses' kind voice in the Vis.

Those infected, desperate, confused people inside the Stadium.

The endless train ride. The excruciating climb up the hill. Nearly dying.

Felix.

Felix.

He said the word 'love', maybe for the first time in his life. She's still scared of that word, even if she's known it longer than him. Who knows what the merc it means, after all? It's forgotten in this cold, mad world they live in. Then she remembers the Clockmaster's blue eyes as he was dying on the snow; her father's brave gaze as he was being tortured on the island; Luke's tears; Jonas' sacrifice. Love. Those things are love.

And more, so much more. Mark's wild expression as she walked into the Stadium.

"You came back for us, Astra? You lovely, incredible girl."

The pride and love shining in his eyes.

The hope on the people's faces as they listened to her tell them they've been fed poison all their lives, they've been fed lies; but Felix Hunter is the cure.

Love.

Felix folding to his knees behind her as she was entering the infected Dome, screaming her name like a wounded animal. Love.

She's not ready to say it yet. Not that she knows what 'belonging' means either. But she knows one thing. Here, with him, it's the first time in her life that she doesn't want to leave. And, the best part?

She's not forced to leave, either. She can stay. She can belong. She can live. She's allowed to.

Who knew that one day that would happen for her? Who knew it was possible?

She's been trying to teach the tin soldier so many things, but she needs to learn, too. By the looks of it, he's one step ahead of her. In some things at least. Her skin heats up, in spite of the freezing cold.

"What are you thinking about, tin soldier?"

Felix has that faraway look in his eyes, a small frown between his eyebrows. His brilliant blue eyes turn to her and his face lights up.

"What else?" he replies. "You."

It wasn't possible. Of course it wasn't possible for her to stay, to belong, to live before he came along. He not only literally saved her life, but he's making the world into a place she can exist in.

He may be staring at her with stars in his eyes, as if she's the wonder who changed it all, but that's not true. *He*'s the wonder. He's the miracle. He woke up and he listened and he was transformed. He walked into certain death. He kissed her in the Stadium. He commanded Kun's soldiers, and they obeyed. He forgave the traitor. He led his own cadets to battle. He made it all happen.

When she first met him he was just a tall, talented, obedient boy. Now... now he's a man. His hair is growing out, his clothes are ripped, his skin sun burnt. His fingers are long and calloused tangled in her hair. His chest rises and falls with each heartbeat. His eyes are vibrant, alive. Awake.

And one more thing.

They're happy. Just like hers.

Oh yes, 'belong' definitely is the word.

twenty-three

He didn't think he could ever utter a word after what she said, but he does -a few minutes later. Or maybe a few hours. He brings a hand to her head and lays his fingers lightly on her drying curls, and says:

"Never say you belong to me, or I to you, match girl. We're done with belonging to another on this Planet. But yes, we belong together. That's a truth that will never change, no matter what happens."

"Is that...?" her voice trails into silence, the question unfinished.

"Yeah?" he prods her on, sitting up.

"Is that how I hurt you when I left?" she repeats in a quiet voice. He goes absolutely still. "The same way she... *they* hurt me every time they left me behind? My father and Urania?"

"Ash, you know I didn't mean..." He swallows.

Her every word pierces his heart. Merc, things were so much easier when he didn't have one.

"Seems to me," she goes on, licking her lips. He raises himself on his elbows to meet her gaze, as she's lying on the floor, and sees that she's swallowing a tear that's slid down to her mouth. His throat hurts again. "Seems to me that people sucked at belonging to each other anyway, maybe even before the pills. Sucked at taking care of each other... at..." A slow blush spreads its way across her neck. "At loving, whatever *that* means."

Felix lifts a hand to touch her wet cheek. His fingers are shaking.

She won't look at him.

"It kills me," he whispers, "when you do that."

She wipes the tears angrily away. "She just... she isn't what I expected," she says. "Urania. Shooting Malik like that... that's what my father fought against. The Rebels... I grew up being taught forgiveness and equality for all. I grew up with a father who was a hero, but almost entirely absent from my life, and a mother who... Well, she was there, but I didn't know it. How could they ever hope to change the world if they didn't consider the one human they created together important enough? Isn't that what you said? That you weren't important enough for me to stay? That's what I've been thinking my entire life, about myself. That I wasn't good enough for them to stay."

Felix pulls her to him fiercely and presses her head against his chest, as her body shakes with silent, dry sobs that steal her breath.

"I'm here, match girl," he says. "There's not going to be any leaving you behind where I'm concerned; I won't last a day without you, we both know that. As long as you don't run again..."

"That's why he died, you know that, right?"

"What?" he asks.

"Jo... Jonas," she says. It takes effort to get his name out. "You were standing there, all frozen, your face looking blank like a carp's. He died so that I wouldn't die, so that you would keep fighting."

Felix leans a step back, swallowing hard. *Jonas... What did you do? Why? For a worthless Drone?* He can't believe it. "Did you say 'carp's'?" he says, trying to steady his voice.

"Well, a bit less lively," Astra replies quietly, but he knows for once she's not making fun of him; her heart is breaking for the Rebel boy. And so is his.

"Look, I still can't believe that Jonas... that he's just gone. His loss was so unnecessary, such a waste. The idea of any of those brilliant, brave Rebels dying is abhorrent, but that boy..." He shakes his head. "Every time I think of it, it's like someone punches me in the stomach. I can't imagine how much you're hurting," he turns to her. "If I could have taken his place and died for you, I'd have done it in a second. He was far more worthy of life than I."

"You always were stupi-"

"Astra, stop it, I'm serious. I'm nothing compared to them. Nothing. At least, if I'd died for you, that would have been the first good thing I did. Something worthwhile, you know?"

"What are you say..." Astra's jaw is hanging open, she can't even get the words out.

"I'm saying that I am, or I was, part of the regime that killed him. I nearly was one of Kun's personal guards; I would have been one of them, if it wasn't for you and the Clockmaster and Ursa. Ash, how can you bear to even look at me? How can you let me come near you, when he is gone? When I first met the Rebels, I couldn't believe people like that existed in the One World. No wonder you wanted to be with them, no wonder you belong with them. And now... to have destroyed one of them, to have..."

He's not allowed to continue.

"I'm sorry, ok?" It bursts out of her with such force, he's taken aback. He stays silent, letting her speak. Her voice gets loud, angry, frustrated. She's holding back tears, and he can't stand to witness such pain. "I'm sorry! Of course you're not worthless. You... you are everything. I should never have left, I thought it was the right thing to do, I only wanted to help you, to give you space to become what you have become... Although I never expected you to become so..."

So... what? So stupid? So awkward? So ignorant? So awesome? So strong? So charming? Give me something here, match girl. He lifts an eyebrow, but she doesn't finish the phrase. *Merc take it.*

Astra is stubbornly sniffling back tears. "I'm sorry for leaving you that first time. I had to. But I'm sorry." She looks down, looking uncomfortable for the first time since he met her.

Felix finds himself hiding a sudden smile. There's no need for apologies, she's already got his whole heart. But he'll be merked if he doesn't drag this out for as long as he can.

"What about the second?"

"That, too," she replies under her breath.

"So you wanted to stay?"

She lifts her wet eyes to his, and suddenly it's not funny at all. "I did," she says. "I didn't know that you weren't like... them." Like Urania and Steadfast. Like everyone who's ever left her behind.

"I'll never leave you," he says, choking up again. "Not willingly."

"Yeah, fine, whatever," Astra says, but she turns her face away, so that he won't see the tears shining in her eyes.

"Hey." He places a finger underneath her chin and tips her face up to his. "Astra. Look at me. There's nothing to forgive. I'm in awe of your bravery, your kindness, your warm, beating heart. I'm wondering what you're doing here with me, when you could have your pick from anyone in the One World."

The sniffling stops. "Nothing is going to happen, match girl -I'm just still reeling from almost losing you, you know? Don't hurt, I can't stand it."

"But something *is* going to happen," she replies. "A lot of somethings, if you have anything to say about it. I mean, what you did with those boys..." She pauses.

"What."

Here it comes.

"Well, it was pretty good. For a tin soldier." She's still looking away from him.

A compliment? That's new. His heart flutters so hard, he's worried it will leap out of his chest. A laugh escapes his lips. "You think so?"

"Don't look so pleased with yourself," she says dryly. His eyebrows draw together, because she might be pretending they aren't there, but her eyes are still full of tears. "You'd blown it several times over by the end. I'm just saying, I know it's not going to be easy and it's not going to be fun, well, not always, but I... I can't believe that you-"

"We," he corrects her.

"We finally started it."

"Oh."

Oh. So those are happy tears running down her cheeks. It's still not easy for him to watch, but he just runs his forefinger down her wet cheek and doesn't say anything else, gulping down his own emotion.

"It could be worse, you know," he says slowly, his fingers playing idly with the end of her braid.

It's curling as it dries out, and he wraps it round his second finger, running his thumb over it. "You could be stuck watching somebody who's hurting because of things you can't change, and your insides could be ripped apart because you can't do a damn thing to take their pain away."

"Somebody who?"

"Somebody..." His lips twitch before forming the word. "Somebody you love."

There's silence for a bit. Silence crackling in the still air; the storm is howling outside.

"Wrong again." The words come out of her so quietly he almost doesn't catch them.

"Yeah," he says, hanging his head. "I know. You've watched your father being... hurt so many times."

He almost said tortured, but stopped himself just in time.

"I can't even imagine how that must have felt," he says. "And then, after being stuck in the Box for such a merking long time, you had to share this tiny shack with a Drone, one of those who were responsible for your father's death. And now, I've changed, but I'm still the person who did all these things. I'm still a little bit blind and a little bit ignorant and a whole lot of stupid. I didn't even think of going into the Dome like you did. I'm not like... I mean, I'm not one of the Rebels. I will never measure up."

She's shaking her head before he's done talking.

"No," she says. "No, you idiot. You've got it all wrong. I don't see you like that, I... never did, that's the truth. In spite of what I kept saying about you being a Drone and stuff like that." She stops to take a deep breath.

He watches her carefully.

He's never seen this side of her, so vulnerable, so raw; she's always the one who knows things he's never even thought of, she's always laughing at him, challenging him. He remembers how, even in the ice, while she was drowning, her eyes seemed to mock his limitations. But now she looks so small in her torn, bloodied clothes, like a child. She's breathing hard, struggling to find the words, and there's color on her cheeks, her little face pinched in concentration. His own chest feels like lead.

She opens her lips again. "And would you stop being jealous of the Rebels? They're my family, they're what I'd die for, but... I meant you."

"Eh?" He wasn't expecting that.

"I was talking about you," she repeats, finally lifting her eyes, looking straight into his. His breath catches. "I thought you'd finally succeeded in breaking that empty head of yours while you were punching Kun back there. It destroyed me to watch you being hurt, being in danger. I mean, my whole life, I have been steeped in loss. My father, the Rebels, I've lost everything and everyone. And today, if I had lost my life, that loss wouldn't have been in vain. Because of you. Because you would still be here, and that's all that matters. But your loss... I wouldn't have recovered from that. It would have killed me. None of us would have recovered, you are the most... Hey, what are you laughing about?"

He's not laughing exactly.

He's sort of laughing and crying and crushing her to him all at once. "I'm here," he says to her. To himself as well. *She was talking about me.* "I'm here, match girl. No more loss."

A few moments pass like this.

He rummages in the cupboards and finds some kind of timer medicine -he refuses to swallow any more Health Discs. Astra takes it from his fingers and he watches her as she ties up his arm, although he can do it himself, but he pretends he can't.

"Do you want to sleep?" he asks her afterwards.

"I don't want to," she replies, "but I guess I should. You, too. Look at you, you're a mess. Have you eaten *anything* since I left?"

He shrugs. "How could I?"

"You've chewed your lips down to the bone, for one thing," she replies, watching him.

He just looks at her for a second. "My..." It's hard to speak. "My insides were draining out," he says.

"That doesn't even *mean* anything." She sounds mad again. Also, like she's about to cry. Maybe that's what's making her mad.

He turns his head aside, taking a sharp breath. His lips curl around a smile, and he lifts a hand to wipe his eyes. He really must be an idiot, like she keeps telling him. How could he not have realized it before now? How can it have taken so long to sink in?

What she's really telling him is that she's been watching him. Even before he woke up, even before he could really see her, she noticed everything about him: when he was hurting and when he was sad and confused. She felt his pain. That's what she's saying. She's also saying she loves him.

She's telling him she loves him. She's *been* telling him she loves him. And he's been too dense to understand.

Who knows how long she's been telling me?

Ever since she ran into the Dome to finish what he started? Ever since she stepped in front of him, so that the taser would attach to her skin instead of his? Ever since she shielded him with her body? Ever since she ran away to the Rebels, so that he'd be forced to become a fighter?

Astra stands up slowly, as though her limbs are aching, and Felix quickly reaches a hand to place under her elbow, to support her.

"I'm fine," she says, pushing him aside. "Got a bit sick of all the... crying and being pathetic down there." He chortles as she moves her hand in the air, gesturing to the floor. "Come on." She heads for the door.

Felix braces his hands on the floor and jumps to his feet to follow.

He just stands in the empty room for a moment, rolling back and forth on the balls of his feet. Even the air smells different in here. It smells of wet hair and smiles, of kisses and plans.

"What is *taking* you so long, soldier boy?" Astra's voice echoes, already muffled by distance - she's climbing down the stairs to the Library.

Felix runs to the loose floorboard and clambers past her, almost running her over in his hurry to overtake her. He's careful that she won't fall, but as soon as he rights her, he runs down past her. She squeals, letting out a sound that's half laughter and half indignation. He leaps the last five stairs down to the ground, then steps towards the switches' panel on the wall. In a second, the Library sparkles into life, hundreds of lights turning on overhead.

"Too slow, match girl," he yells, hurrying towards the Pantry arch.

Astra's steps are hurrying behind him, the sounds of her socks padding on the steps.

He slows down a bit, waiting for her to catch up. They reach the arch together, and he slides an arm carelessly across her shoulders as they roam the shelves, looking for something new to eat.

"You want to go sit in the stupid fire-room, don't you?" Felix tells her as soon as they pop a box of 'noodle soup' -whatever *that* is- on the heater. Of course, he has to run back upstairs and get the heater, because he forgot it in his hurry, and Astra nearly busts a lung laughing at him.

"*You*'re stupid," she says. "And it's 'Christmas'. The Christmas room."

"That's the one," Felix says, resigned to his fate. "Tell you what, if you're a good girl, I'll even turn the PR fire thingy on. I might even read you a story."

"You're so full of yourself, you know that? Besides, I'm not going to be a good girl, I can tell you right now," Astra replies.

"Oh, I'm counting on it," Felix says, and before she realizes what's happening, he's put an arm around her knees and is lifting her over his head, balancing her weight on his shoulders. She lets out a shriek that will probably leave him hearing-impaired for life, her braid swinging wildly into his eyes. He lowers her until her waist is level with his face, then twirls her around.

"Put me down, you crazy boy," she says. "The food will burn."

"Everything will burn," he says against her neck in a husky, gruff voice, sliding her down across his body until he can bury his face in her hair. "Everything you touch, Astra. Match girl."

"So we'll start a fire," she says, her eyes turning serious.

"Burn the wrong, build the new, isn't that what the Rebels say?"

"More or less," she smiles, which, smile, means that he totally butchered the saying. She gets what he wanted to say, though. "Peace on earth and all that," she says.

"Goodwill to men," he supplies.

"Right," Astra replies. "So, let's get on with it. Work to do."

"Whatever you say," Felix sets her on her feet and sweeps a mock bow to the floor before turning to the shelves to grab two bowls.

twenty-four

As soon as their bowls are filled with steaming, fragrant soup, Astra sits cross-legged in the middle of the carpet of the Pantry Arch, gazing up at the packed shelves with thousands of labels. The Christmas room is on the other side of the Library, and she can see that Felix is ready to drop, so she doesn't insist that they walk all the way down the hall to eat.

It feels so strange to be back down here, after all that's happened. Nothing has changed inside this Arch's room. And everything is different.

"So," she starts saying just as Felix starts slurping his food loudly and making satisfied grunts. "Kun was planning on delivering a virus-ridden Planet to the Venus Commander."

"Is that what you want to talk about right now?" Felix asks, his brow furrowing as he puts the bowl down and blows on his fingers -they're burnt. He picks it up again and attacks the food with all his might.

Astra smiles at him only after he's turned his attention to his bowl again. "Yep. I need to get this straight. He got Ulysses-"

"His father," Felix interrupts, and she can sense him tense up, his muscles coiling, his shoulders going taut.

"He got his father to help him with the Clock ceremony, because he had you in the Box. He was blackmailing him all these years?" She asks.

Felix doesn't speak. Astra sets her food aside. He's stopped eating, too, and turns his back to her slightly.

"Then, right before executing you," she goes on, "you were freed, yes? Ulysses did that, that's why you rushed to this place when the Vis came, even though you were just a quiet, obedient little tin soldier. You owe him."

"My life," Felix says.

She swallows. "Still, it was a pretty gutsy thing to do, for a Drone."

"Enough with the flattery." Felix lifts his bowl in the air and drains it in one gulp. Then he gets up and starts looking longingly at the boxes on the shelves. "Hey, do you know what 'pheasant' is? I mean, it was a timer beast, but why the stars is it in a box in the Pantry?"

She ignores him. "Kun freed you in exchange for the twenty-f..." She stumbles over the number.

"Twenty-five twenty-four," he says, quietly.

"That one. Last year's Clock. The one that would release the virus in little droplets all over the stadium. Infecting about... a hundred and..."

"Not a hundred," he corrects. "The stadium holds approximately two hundred thousand people. You know how much that is?"

She nods. "A lot," she says. "Then they'd go back to their continents, infecting everyone around them within days, and in a few months' we'd all be dead. Except for Kun. He must have been promised some kind of high military position in the Venus Colony; what do you think it was?" He shrugs. "But, tell me this," she goes on. "In a few months' time, why wouldn't we ask Mars' Command- Urania," she swallows, "for the cure?"

"Why would we?" he replies. "And even if we did, you saw how... reluctant she was to help." He winces, but she doesn't say anything, because what is there to say? "For all Kun knew, she had no reason to ally her Planet with Earth. For all anyone knew."

"The Rebels knew, though," she says. "Matt told me while I was inside. He... you know the Rebels are Elite, right? Or at least they used to be."

At this he turns around, his face blank.

"What did you say?" His eyes are round with surprise, his face gone completely white. He looks like he's about to crumple.

Oh, so he didn't know.

"The Rebels are members of the Elite. They all left high-paying jobs to form the resistance. They're some of the best educated and most skilled mechanics and nano-scientists on the Planet. My father was, too. Matt, Luke, all of them. I thought Urania, or Ruth, as she was called then, was the only one who was a simple girl like me, rescued from the Worker Settlements, but it turns out she was so much more..."

"Don't think about her, Ash," Felix says in a broken voice. "Please."

She smiles bitterly. As if she can stop thinking about her. It's incredible to her though, that he wants to protect her from the pain. Such a contrast to that time he just stood by, coolly, as she watched her father being tortured to pieces on the PR. Now his arm muscles ripple as he clenches his fist.

But the truth is, he can't protect her from this. No more than she can protect him from the unfairness of it all, from the heavy burden that's fallen on his shoulders. Sometimes, pain is the only way to change.

"Urania is who I came from," she replies. "Just like Kun is who you came from. If we don't think about them, we won't ever be able to be better than them."

Felix scoffs. "Better?" he repeats with a small laugh. "You're already better than ten Mars Commanders, match girl."

She smiles. *Do you really think so?* she wants to ask him, but if he didn't think so then why would he say it and so she leaves it alone.

"Anyway, I was trying to say that my guess is your job will be much easier if you want to trust the Rebels...They know things, they knew how to get into the Dome, and so much more. Listen to them."

"No."

He whirls around so quickly, she stumbles back. He takes a step towards her, looming a full head above her, and grabs her wrist in a blood-stopping grasp. "No," he repeats, his eyes spitting fire.

"No what?" she asks.

"It's not my job." He lets go of her hand, and sits down beside her.

He threads an arm around her shoulders, cradling her neck in the crook of his elbow, tucking her to his chest. She feels his lips brush the top of her head.

She must look a mess, her hair a dried-up tangle, frizzy curls escaping every which way, probably getting into his lips. She tries to wiggle out, but he tightens his arm around her.

"It's ours," he says, and his voice sounds a little shaky. *What now?* He swallows, his Adam's apple bobbing above her head. "It's *our* job. If... if you want it to be." Pause. "Please," he adds, in a whisper.

"I did say you're an idiot," Astra replies. She clears her throat -it was closing up for some reason. "And you're more stupid than I thought if you even have to wonder if I'll be by your side." He won't let her move away from his arms, but to be honest, she doesn't want to.

"I don't just want you by my side," he says. "I want you to..." He stops. Tries again. "I want..." His breath is coming too short, he has to stop once more.

Astra waits.

"I know," she murmurs after a few seconds pass and he can't find the words. "Just keep in mind that I'm not like you, I've had practically no education, no training, I don't-"

Her phrase is cut off by his lips pressing into her mouth. He opens them, teasing her tongue with his, and kisses her deeply, breathlessly. He presses her close and they stay like this, their bodies entwined, their lips exchanging words without words.

"Do you think we can win?" she asks him as soon as they part.

"I love you," he says. The blue of his eyes is brilliant, blinding.

"Do you think our forces could ever be a match for theirs?" she insists. "Do you think maybe... maybe there's something on Earth that they're afraid of, and that's why they wanted to force the Planet to surrender without a war?"

He looks away from her briefly, keeping his eyes shut for a second. When he opens them next, their shine is gone.

"I know for a fact that there's something on Earth they're scared of," he says. "You." She inhales sharply, untangling herself from his arms. This isn't what she meant...

Felix catches her against him, forcing her to look up at him. "Think about it," he says, "what Steadfast kept saying during the Fortnight of Terror. The one word that had the Counsil so scared they lied to the military for all these years. They had the entire military force looking for you. 'Astra'. His daughter. His weapon. His hope."

Astra blinks a few times. "'*Felix, my hope*'. Ulysses' last words. We were their last hope."

"No," Felix says. "It's you. You are what they're afraid of. You are the reason for our alliance with Mars. You are the reason Steadfast and the Rebels fought for a better world -for his daughter who would inherit it. And..."

"And?"

A slow smile spreads across his face, and he trails a long finger across the line of her jaw. "And his daughter's," he says softly. "And the daughter of her daughter. And so on."

t w e n t y - f i v e

Astra can't speak. She's shaking, thinking of the Gangs in the Box.

Felix goes on. "Just think about it. What better motive could there have been for Steadfast than this: Create a world where his daughter can live safely and have happy little red-haired babies and learn the Greek wisdom his father had preserved, and have everything else her heart desires."

His voice has taken on a dreamy expression. He's half-closed his eyes and is frowning slightly. *Is he dreaming of her father's motives or his own?*

Astra has a hard time concentrating on what he's saying. *He doesn't know*, she screams inside. *He doesn't know what they did to me in the Box.*

He can't imagine it. All they took from us. He'll never know how they killed me every time a Guard walked into our cell and picked one of us for their experiments; every time they forced me watch an execution; every time I looked into my father's eyes as he was tortured on the PR screen, broadcast for the entire world to rewatch again and again.

"Hey."

Felix has stopped talking. He's looking at her.

"Hey," he says again, and his expression changes. His hands start moving down her back in a circular motion, warm, steady, and she can breathe again. "Whatever you're thinking, stop it." He grabs her elbow and brings her so close to him, she has to tip her head up to look into his face. He swallows. "Stop it, now."

"It's all right," she says, hoping he can't tell how it hurts just to get the words out right now. "I was just... remembering things."

"I promise," he says in a hoarse, husky voice. "I promise you, match girl. Your father's sacrifice wasn't in vain. Nor will yours be. That's all I've been thinking about since... since I lost you. Or I thought I did. While I was at Headquarters, making decisions, giving out orders and, stars help me, hardly knowing what I was doing, this was the only thing I could think of coherently."

"What?"

"How I wouldn't, I *won't* let all you did, all you've suffered be in vain. All you've lost."

He's saying exactly what she's thinking. Her skin is covered in goose bumps. She shivers.

"I kept thinking about how I'll fight with all I've got to make this world right for you. Or, at least, to make you happy."

Everything slows down, stills. Her mind empties of all the dark thoughts, all the evil memories.

"What did you say?"

"To make you happy," Felix repeats obediently. He looks at her with a question in his eyes, wondering what she doesn't get. "What? Why are you looking at me like I-?"

And then he gets it and he stops talking. A huge smile spreads across his lips, stretching the planes of his face, reaching all the way to his chiseled cheekbones.

"Match girl," his voice drops, it sounds like a caress. Like a kiss. "Match girl, Astra, look at me. Has no one ever said that to you before? Has no one ever fought an army just so they could make sure you'd be safe and happy? Has no one...?"

And now it's her turn to shut him up, because if he goes on like this, she'll turn into a sobbing mess. So she does the only thing left to do under the circumstances.

She hugs him back, her arms a tight circle around his waist, and buries her face into his chest.

He freezes stiff for a second, taken aback. Then, with a sigh, he pulls her close, tightening his hold on her, and melts into her.

twenty-six

"They'll always be in awe of our Planet," Felix says, "because that's where everything started. Water, air -even their DNA. The very matter they are made of comes from Earth. We may be a poor Planet, a destroyed, ravaged world; but we sure as Jupiter can survive. We survived the Romans, the Flood, the Great Wars, all three of them; we survived the After Plague. We survived Kun. Just barely, but we did. How can anyone not be afraid of that?"

"How indeed," she murmurs absently. "Felix?"

"Yeah?" He shudders against her as she says his name, sending a ripple of delicious tingles all over her skin.

"You know I have no idea what half those things you said mean."

"I don't either," he laughs. "Just showing off. But that's ok, we'll learn. Do you think any of the Colonies have a Library of Truth?"

She shakes her head against his shoulder.

"That's our strongest weapon then. I really have got to start with the Greeks," he mumbles under his breath. "Also, I saw a box named 'jam' in there."

Ah, still thinking about food. That's her tin soldier.

"Think it might be another powerful, new weapon?"

She can't help it; she bursts out laughing. They used to make compost jam in the mountains from all the fresh fruit and harvest products. Jam is one thing she knows everything about.

"I wouldn't be surprised if it was," she says.

When they untangle themselves, reluctantly, Felix gets up gingerly and hands her a plate full of steaming liquid that smells like happiness and safety. Oh, it's her own bowl of soup, still full; he's rewarmed it.

"Ok, time to feed you," he says. "Here, don't burn your fingers like I did. Wait, hey, what-?"

But she's already up and running down the hall to the Arts arch, a bit of soup sloshing out the sides of the warm bowl as she runs.

"Taking it in!" She yells, not waiting to see if he follows. Behind her Felix gives out a long-suffering sigh that sounds suspiciously like a giggle, and then his steps echo across the archway as he follows.

She walks into the Christmas room and presses her hand to the wall. One by one the tree lights start to glow. Then the fireplace stimulation turns on in the PR, then the fairy lights looping around the bookshelves. She buries herself in the afghan that's still on the armchair, and that's how Felix finds her when he walks in.

He just sort of freezes in the archway, and goes pale. Then tears start coursing down his cheeks.

He's definitely lost weight, she thinks, watching him sway against the arch frame. How did she not notice before now? It's the first time she's taken a proper look at him. His cheekbones weren't as pronounced before, nor was there any soft stubble on his chin. He looks impossibly tall standing there below the arch. His hair is drying wildly around his head, the white streak in the front flopping down his forehead, brushing his eyelashes. His lips are parted, shaking slightly, and that breaks her heart more than the sight of his eyes all swollen and red, or the bluish circles underneath them.

He just stands there, frozen, as though he's forgotten how to inhale.

"Felix? What is it?" she says, quickly setting the soup down and getting to her feet. She runs over and stands next to him, but he's looking straight ahead, unseeing, his eyes turning glassy. "What's wrong? Did I do something?"

A hand brings her forcibly to his chest, and she feels his heart beat against her ear. She can hardly breathe, he's crushing her to his body so hard, pushing his lips against her temple.

She lets herself fold into him, taking in his boy-smell, the snow and blood on his clothes. The lean, hard muscles that crush her arms.

"Don't be sad," she mumbles against his shirt, aching at the thought of how it must have been for him, passing by this arch every day, almost seeing her seated there, and knowing she left him, willingly, after all they'd been through together. Great. Now she's sniffling too. "I really shouldn't have left you. But in my defense," she adds in a small voice, "I didn't know you... cared so much."

"Liar," his voice, gruff, says from above her head. "You knew how much I cared from the moment I took off my gear so I could grab you from the water in that black hole. I lost both my goggles and my gloves that day. Not to mention my dignity."

"Like you ever had any to begin with," she chokes against his chest. His hands are circling her waist, resting lightly across her stomach, and sending ripples of heat all over her body. She's shaking, and it's not from cold or fatigue this time. Felix shudders against her, his long body hard and strong as they stand there, pressed together, fairy lights and food forgotten.

Well, this isn't fair, she thinks. That's such a strange thought to strike her at that moment, yet it is what passes through her mind. How unfair it all is. She's never complained, never grumbled about losing her father. But now it quietly strikes her, how he should be here.

That he should be seeing her happy, and loved, and fighting his fight. He should be the one helping Felix; he's the only one who can. He was the only one who could.

His absence hits her like a wave.

Father, she thinks. She can think of him now, here, she can pretend to talk to him as if he was there, like she used to do before he died. His absence doesn't tear her apart, not like it did before. She can't fall apart with Felix's arms around her, can she? He won't let her. So she talks to him, in her head.

I'm not sure I can do this without you. I don't even know how to read, for merc's sake. But we started something, something good maybe, so we'll see it through. Watch over us. I'll do the best I can -I'm sure he will too. And everyone who wakes up and sees the truth will do the same.

Not everyone wants to wake up, I know that, but I have and he has, and there's no turning back now.

I'll fight with all I've got, and change all I can, and then I'll close my eyes and come to meet you. Then let the Maker of the universe decide.

"I know you miss your father," Felix says, out of the blue, as if he can hear her thoughts. Then again, he always could tell what she was thinking. It's irritating. Then his voice starts sounding choked with emotion again, and something sharp pinches her heart. "I kind of miss him too, although I never knew him. I know I'll never be like Steadfast, but I…"

"You'll be better," Astra interrupts him. "You already are, in a sense: you're here. And you're fighting to stay. That's enough for now, for me. You… you do know I care about you, right?" His eyes find hers, impossibly blue, shining with unshed tears. "I mean, as much as I know how to care-"

"You know plenty." He sniffles. "For example, you know there's no chance on mars that I'll ever deserve you."

"Don't be ridiculous."

"I mean it, Ash. I know what I am and where I come from. How can you love me?" She gives him a sharp look. "Sorry, sorry," he backs away a step. "I shouldn't be saying it, when you haven't even…"

She takes a deep breath. "Well, anyway, I do."

"What?" His left eyebrow rises almost to his hairline.

"Must I say it?" she asks, hoping she'll sound more annoyed than scared -which she is how she actually feels. "The actual words?"

"You must," he says, in a maddening, calm way.

Oh, stars take it. "I love you," she tells him. And it doesn't feel scary, now that she's said it.

"Finally," he says infuriatingly, and she raises her fist to his cheek, but he laughs and tucks her into his arms, pressing her to his chest until she feels her bones will melt. "Finally, she said it," he repeats, his voice catching.

twenty-eight

After they eat, they get sleepy. Felix folds his long body under the Christmas tree, and Astra lays her head on his chest. They stay like that a long time, their bodies vertical, listening to each other's heartbeat.

"The Pods are all closed," Felix says at some point.

"I know," she replies. "So?"

"So, I wanted to take you places."

She sits up, only to take a good look at his face. He's serious. She lays back down, and his hand smoothes the hair away from her forehead, as he wiggles to make his chest a comfortable pillow.

"I'm fine with the places I've been," she says.

"What places?" he retorts. He sounds annoyed, almost angry. "The mountains are incredible, I'll give you that. But apart from up there, you've only seen the inside of the Settlemets, the bottom of a freezing lake, and the B-"

He stops himself before he says 'the Box.' And wisely, too. She feels so vulnerable right now, lying on top of him like this, that she'll punch him if he so much as mentions anything from the past.

He exhales loudly. "I wanted to take you to the sea. I wanted you to feel the sun on your face, the sand under your feet." A snort, coming from her, interrupts him. "Laughing at me again, match girl?"

"Well, it's not like you've felt the sun in your face," she says. "Not with that mask covering up everything."

"It's goggles, not a mask."

"Whatever it is, it's stupid." He doesn't say anything else, nor does she. Then, "where would you take me, theoretically speaking?"

He's curling a strand of her hair around his finger. "The Caribbean," he says immediately.

She doesn't know why he would say that; she doesn't know how she feels, hearing it. "No," she says quietly. "Not yet." His hand moves to her shoulder. He squeezes and doesn't let go. "But we still have boats and stuff, right? If I ever felt like it?"

His chest rumbles with silent laughter. "Yes, we still have boats and stuff."

"Cool. It's nice to have the option, that's all. I've never had that before."

"A boat?"

"An option. To do something or not. I was always forced to... Never mind." She shrugs, looking up at the cuckoo clocks. A few of them are working correctly, she notices. They show the same hour. Felix must have fixed them before he left for the Perennial; he sure as merc figured everything out, just as she knew he would. It's almost dawn.

Outside the shack, the sky's blackness will be breaking soon. The dawn will paint the sky pale pink. And somewhere out there, Ursa is running free, wild. Ursa, their protector, their friend. Their future. She was the one who started their story, the one who brought them together, and she finished it. She is part of the hope for a new, living world.

"Ash?" Felix's breathing has gotten so rhythmic, she thought he'd fallen asleep. His voice sounds rough, groggy.

"Yeah?"

"Are you asleep?"

"Not yet, but I think you are."

"Nah, don't think so." He moves, bending his leg under her knee. He turns his head into her hair. "If I'm asleep, how come I'm not dreaming you're telling me you love me over and over again?"

Astra doesn't know if she should laugh or elbow him. In the end, she does neither.

She lifts a hand and pushes the hair away from his eyes. "I love you," she whispers close to his lips. "Now shut up and sleep, we have to get up in a bit."

"Match girl," he murmurs in his sleep, and there's a world of tenderness in these two words.

An entire world.

twenty-nine

tin soldier

Felix feels like a king, hearing those words on her lips again. Sleep overtakes him, even though his brain is too excited to stop working, trying to catch up with the words' new, sweet taste on his mouth.

"Match girl," he murmurs as he sinks into oblivion. *She said the new word. She said it to me.* He asks her to tell him she loves him again, half expecting to be told to shut up.

"I love you," it sounds as if she replies. "I love you," she says again. Then it sounds as if she tells him to shut up and he can feel himself smiling, even in his sleep.

Still half-asleep, Felix turns over and threads his arm through hers. She lets out a sigh, and buries her nose inside the crook of his neck, falling asleep instantly. And just like that, he's wide awake.

He doesn't dare to breathe as he feels her weight on his chest, her body relaxing completely into his. Then he takes a breath slowly, letting the air out, trying to stop himself from hyperventilating. She's right, he'll have to get up in less than an hour.

Stars, he's got so much to do.

He's still got words to learn. Words like freedom and human and rights. Hope and faith and justice. And more, many more than that. He's got books to study, he's got Luke to meet, and the stories of the Old Ones to learn. He's got a world to put back together; he's got himself to build from scratch before he does anything else.

That will take him a lifetime. At least.

But for now, he just lies there, looking at the little rosy cheek that's leaning against his shoulder, watching Astra's chest rise and fall, feeling her heart beat next to his own. His heart. His beating heart.

And that's how it begins, the change.

It doesn't begin in a battlefield, with human beings falling to never get up; it doesn't begin in a glittering auditorium, with the Elite gathered around to watch; it doesn't even begin in the Headquarters Hall, with his soldiers next to him.

It begins with him and her, it begins down here in the Library of Truth, it begins with knowledge. And love.

'Equal in guilt,' Felix remembers the Rebel's words that shook him to his very core.

'*Felix, my hope,*' he remembers the Clockmaster's eyebrows drawing together in the Vis he watched about a thousand times.

'*I love you,*' Astra's voice echoes in his head.

Only now does he recognize what has been happening to him all these days; what was happening to him when he was training his soldiers on the frozen plains, when he was rescuing a girl from a hole in the ice, when he was fighting against his father on the mountain. All those moments were his starting point. They also were his lowest point, from where he can only climb upwards.

So this is how it begins. With Astra, with the shack, with the books and the lights and the boxes of treasures surrounding them. With Ursa watching guard, somewhere out there. With Ulysses' prayers and Ulysses' Vis in his pocket.

It begins with two beating hearts.

Liked it?

Don't forget to review!

Did you know how much a single positive review can help an author out?

If a book has over a certain number of reviews it's automatically bumped up to the retailer's bestseller list!

So just write a few words to show your appreciation for the author's hard work!

NO ORDINARY STAR

NO PLAIN REBEL

The creation of this book would not have been possible without the help of the amazing **tumblr** , **instagram and facebook** community. I went to you guys for support and encouragement, and found inspiration. Special thanks to my NOS street team, you are amazing book warriors and I'd be lost without you.

Not only this book, but also its author wouldn't be here if it wasn't for someone —*my* someone. You are my constant source of strength and happiness. You know who you are to me and why everything I ever write will be dedicated to you.

M.C. FRANK lives with her 'dude' in a home filled with candles, laptops and notebooks, where she rearranges her overflowing bookshelves every time she feels stressed.
Which is often, since (as you might have noticed) she doesn't pick the easiest subjects for her novels.
Learn more about her and her New Adult, Young Adult, Greek mythology and historical novels online.

Find all of M.C. Frank's books on her website:
mcfrankauthor.com

Twitter: **@mcfrank_author**

Instagram: **mcfrank_author**

Tumblr blog: **@mcfrank_author**

Facebook: **M.C. Frank**

Goodreads: **M.C. Frank**

CPSIA information can be obtained
at www.ICGtesting.com
Printed in the USA
LVOW12s0529251117
557519LV00001B/237/P